"Ross, I don't want to talk any more to-night," Sage said firmly. "I've got to get some sleep now. I'm setting the alarm for six-thirty tomorrow."

Ross whistled softly, glancing at the illuminated dial of his watch. "That gives us just four and a half hours, then."

Summer moonlight gave her face a silvery glow as she nodded. Ross felt a shudder run through Sage, and his body moved closer in response. Before either of them sensed what was happening, he bent his head and took her mouth with his.

Sage couldn't stop her hand from coming up to clutch at his waist. She pulled her mouth back a little. "Ross, I don't want—"

"I know," Ross replied with sensual ferocity, covering her lips with his once more, his body shuddering with the intensity of his need for this woman. "You're still fire to me, Sage," he muttered hoarsely.

"Ross," Sage gasped, "let me go."

Fury tamped his ardor as he pulled back from her. "How do you manage it?"

"Manage what?" Sage fought to keep her voice even.

"Refuse me while your body clamors for my caress . . ."

WHAT ARE *LOVESWEPT* ROMANCES?

They are stories of true romance and touching emotion. We believe those two very important ingredients are constants in our highly sensual and very believable stories in the *LOVESWEPT* line. Our goal is to give you, the reader, stories of consistently high quality that may sometimes make you laugh, sometimes make you cry, but are always fresh and creative and contain many delightful surprises within their pages.

Most romance fans read an enormous number of books. Those they truly love, they keep. Others may be traded with friends and soon forgotten. We hope that each *LOVESWEPT* romance will be a treasure—a "keeper." We will always try to publish

*LOVE STORIES YOU'LL NEVER FORGET
BY AUTHORS YOU'LL ALWAYS REMEMBER*

The Editors

LOVESWEPT® • 121

Helen Mittermeyer
Tempest

 BANTAM BOOKS
TORONTO • NEW YORK • LONDON • SYDNEY • AUCKLAND

TEMPEST

A Bantam Book / December 1985

LOVESWEPT® *and the wave device are registered trademarks of Bantam Books, Inc. Registered in U.S. Patent and Trademark Office and elsewhere.*

ISBN 0-553-21734-8

Published simultaneously in the United States and Canada

Bantam Books are published by Bantam Books. Inc. Its trademark. consisting of the words "Bantam Books" and the portrayal of a rooster. is registered in U.S. Patent and Trademark Office and in other countries. Marca Registrada. Bantam Books. Inc.. 666 Fifth Avenue. New York. New York 10103.

PRINTED IN THE UNITED STATES OF AMERICA

O   0 9 8 7 6 5 4 3 2 1

This book is dedicated to Paul Snedden, my cousin, and to all hearing-impaired persons.

To Morris, the wild turkey who lived in Durand Eastman Park in the early 1980s. He had a dignity that made all who knew him love him, even if he did peck the day-lights out of my car.

One

Ross St. John Tempest woke that morning thinking as he usually did of Sage Peters Tempest, his wife. He yawned and swung his legs out of bed, then cursed as he struck his toe. The bed in the gardener's cottage of his parents' estate was too short for his six-feet-four-inch frame. "Damn!" He hopped up and down. If his wife were home with him where she belonged, he would be sleeping in his own mammoth bed in their house, a little more than a mile from his parents' home.

"To hell with you, Sage! I'm getting tired of this merry-go-round," he said aloud. He had called her four or five times trying to learn why Sage was in Rochester, four hundred and fifty miles from their home on Long Island. It was impossible to fathom why she had left in the first place. All that mattered was that she belonged with her husband, not in the woods in upstate New York trying out recipes. When he phoned they had talked of the weather, how they were feeling, and other banal topics. One time they even talked about what she was cooking for dinner that evening . . . as if either one of them cared!

For two pins he'd go up to Rochester and drag her back by the hair! No! Dammit, she had left him . . . Oh, she had described it in her note as putting space between them so she could think about their lives, but hell, it was nothing less than desertion. He glared at the clothes he would wear that day as though they were the offenders, then stalked into the pink-and-brown marble bathroom. The bathroom was hardly a place where he could forget Sage, for they had managed stolen moments at the cottage during their short engagement.

Ross felt alone, threatened, off keel . . . emotions he wasn't used to in the least. He ran a multimillion-dollar conglomerate and did it with ease and enjoyment. It was absurd that he couldn't manage a smooth marriage. He ground his teeth together as he thought of her. He seemed to be angry most of the time.

His mother had told him in flat terms that she wasn't inviting him to dinner again until he became more civilized, after he told one of her darling state senators that he was a pompous ass.

He was furious with Sage and angry at himself because for the first time in his life he felt that he was making all the wrong moves.

He turned on the shower and stood under cold water until goosebumps rose all over his body. He *hadn't* moved out of their spacious home on Long Island because he saw her in every corner, he insisted to himself. It was simply that it was ridiculous for one person to live in such a big house. Of course their apartment in Manhattan, though much smaller, wasn't any better. He forced the thought to submerge. It was just more sensible to stay in the cottage . . . for a while.

He could picture how Sage had looked when he brought her to the cottage the first time. He'd only known her a month. She was almost nineteen and just about to graduate early from college. Oh, she was smart all right, he thought, having started college at sixteen and rushed through in three full years, one of which she had spent in Europe. A reluctant laugh escaped him as he lathered his body: brains, beauty . . . and incredible sexuality. They hadn't been able to keep their hands off each other.

Ross rinsed his head and body, then groped for the outsize bathsheet he'd hung on the rod. Lord, their honeymoon had been incredible. He threw on his clothes, pulling his tie so tight he hurt his throat. When he adjusted the knot in the mirror, he saw the bed behind him and recalled Sage and he locked in embraces there, never seeming to tire of each other. They had lain there entwined, their wedding not three days away, and talked of the children they would have. "I don't want children right away," he'd said. "We need time alone together."

"This way, of course." She had laughed into his shoulder. "Even if we never had children, I would still love you, but I think four is a nice number."

He had smiled and agreed.

"Ha . . ." Ross's scornful laugh echoed now around the room. "So, Sage," he said, "why are you staying in Rochester when you should be back here with your husband? If we want children, we can't do it long-distance." He smothered the small voice deep inside that said he should have given her a week, or two, a month at the most, before following her, but never have waited these eight long months. "It was up to her to come home," he said forcefully. Maybe, he thought, it was time he told her he wanted to try for a family. He shrugged, feeling uncomfortable. For the hundredth time he wondered why she hadn't talked to him. Heaven knew she had a way with words; she'd been so successful in law school, then as a public defender. She could talk about any subject at the dinner parties they'd given, especially after she developed an interest in cooking. They'd entertained enough for her to try out almost every speciality in the Cordon Bleu cookbook. He glowered at himself. Sage had grown aloof, quiet. He felt buffaloed by the ambivalence of guilt and anger warring within him. He shot a last look at the bed and went clumping down the stairs, grabbing for his briefcase. He was still thinking about his relationship with Sage when he arrived thirty minutes late at his office. There was an urgent call from Bonn that he had to take, making him late for the board meeting and, to his mind, putting him at a disadvantage.

He looked around the conference room, noticing that two of the members had pursed lips and three others were biting theirs. Dammit, he didn't need trouble this morning, but he knew he was going to get flak about the Berman construction complex. He would bet every nickel of the Temp Corporation that it would pay off in the long run, but right now it was several million in the red.

He was just about to call the meeting to order when he heard a disturbance at the door. He felt his mouth go slack when he saw his secretary being towed into the room by a burly man with an envelope in his hand.

"What the hell—" Ross began.

"I called security, sir," his secretary said.

"Are you Ross St. John Tempest?" the stranger asked.

"Yes, but who the hell are you?

"You are hereby served," the man said flatly, and handed Ross the envelope.

*   *   *

Ross Tempest was in a mood that matched his last name. How dare Sage have him served with separation papers! When the hell did she get so nervy? He had put up with her fits and starts of rebellion. In fact he had encouraged her to become her own woman. He didn't like clinging females; they annoyed him. But he could not tolerate her audacity in serving him with papers, and in his own conference room to boot. He hit the steering wheel with his fist. He blinked through his fury and realized that he was exceeding the speed limit by thirty miles an hour and that he wasn't noting any of the landmarks that he should have been.

He had been to Rochester once before when Sage's aunt had been alive, but usually Sage had visited her relative by herself. The press of business usually had him tied up. She had seemed content with that. "Dammit, why shouldn't she be content?" They had married the day after Sage had graduated from Sarah Lawrence, and though she had been nervous at first about fitting in with his high-powered family, things had worked out . . . or so it seemed to him. Admittedly the honeymoon bloom was off their union, but he had never strayed—and dammit he could have. Now—he hit the steering wheel again—she had the gall to have him served with papers that could ultimately lead to their divorce. . . .

He almost missed his turn off the expressway, he was so taken up with his thoughts. She had betrayed him!

He saw the sign for the town she lived in, Irondequoit, and scowled at it. What had made her come back to live here anyway? They had a lovely home on Long Island, a host of friends, an active social life. They were free to come and go as they pleased, no children to encumber them. They took interesting vacations at least twice a year. What the hell else did she want? Ross fumed.

He followed the curving road through the woodsy area of the town of some fifty thousand that abutted the city of Rochester, not able to admire the parklike setting of the area. He knew, from what Sage had told him, that deer and other animals roamed freely in the area and that the lovely, gracious homes seemed to sit in very private lots, close enough to neighbors for comfort, but isolated from the noise of highways and the crush of people that Ross had always found soothing. He loved the hum of the city. Sage didn't, but that had been a small difference between them.

He slowed his speed on the curving road as the homes became more scattered, the woods thicker. He saw the sign ARBOR LANE and made a turn onto the meandering road that wasn't much more than a single-car driveway in width. There was only one house on Arbor Lane and that had belonged to Sage's Aunt Elizabeth Peters, who had been married to Sage's uncle. There had been no children and it had been a natural thing for Elizabeth Peters to adopt Sage when her parents had died in an auto accident. Ross had rather liked the crusty old lady, who had died of heart disaese more than three years ago, but he had urged Sage to sell the home in upstate New York, not able to see a use for it in their lives. Sage had refused.

He was about to park the Cadillac he'd leased in front of the two-car garage when something coming out of the wooded area next to the house caught his attention. "What the hell!" he exclaimed as a red-crested two-legged creature that looked like a small ostrich came on the run at the car, gobbling in anger. Ross watched, more annoyed than worried, when the creature began pecking at the shiny paint job on the Eldorado. Ross was about to open his door when the creature attacked the driver's window. More irritated now, Ross pushed open the car door, ready to wring the bird's neck, when he heard a high-pitched, unnatural voice behind him. He turned and saw a boy waving his hands.

"Naw-ty tur-key. Naw-ty Mor-r-ris," the boy said in a high-pitched monotone.

Ross knew at once the boy was hearing impaired. He had hearing-impaired people working at his plant in New Jersey and had dealt with them frequently.

"Hello."

"Hel-lo, Sor-ry a-bout Mor-ris. He does-n't like cars."

"I can see that. He's a wild turkey, isn't he?"

The boy nodded and smiled, patting the bird, who had trotted to his side and was pecking at his shirt. "He thinks he's the head ma-an around he-re."

Ross smiled. He knew enough about the handicap to realize that at some time the youngster had had hearing. Though his speech was high and monotone, the good syllable use pointed to hearing at some level of understanding. When suddenly a big golden retriever came round the car barking, Ross stepped between it and the boy. "Watch out."

"That's ju-ust Midas, my dog."

The dog sniffed at Ross and gave a cautious wag of his tail.

Ross liked dogs, but he had always felt that he and Sage were too busy to own one. He patted the dog's head and in return he received another slow wag of the tail. He noted that the dog placed himself close to and in front of the boy. "I know the dog's name and the turkey's name, but I don't know yours."

The boy grinned. "My name's Tad, for Thom-as Andr-ew Peters."

Ross couldn't prevent the start of surprise. He couldn't recall Sage ever talking about a relative who had children this age.

"And"—the boy took a deep breath and swallowed as though talking had been difficult for him, then pointed

behind Ross—"that's my sis-ter, Pip, for Phil-lip-a
Pe-ters. She can-n't talk."

Ross swiveled to look at the slight girl, her blond hair
in pigtails, her eyes blue, huge, and fixed intently on
him. Then he looked back at the boy, aware that he had
to face a lip-reader directly. "You both have blond hair
and blue eyes . . . and you're going to be tall." It flashed
through his mind that they had Sage's coloring.

Tad grinned and nodded. Pip edged around to stare at
Ross while stroking the dog, which had moved to her
side.

When the wild turkey approached the girl, Ross
stiffened, then watched as the small-boned child
reached out and patted the neck of the strutting animal.
He exhaled a deep breath. He turned back to Tad and
said distinctly, "I'm looking for the woman who lives in
this house. A Mrs. Tempest?"

Tad watched his mouth very carefully, then nodded.
"My . . . moth-er."

Ross felt as though someone had punched him in the
stomach. There was a mistake obviously! "You must
have misunderstood me." He enunciated each word,
realizing that lip-reading was a very difficult thing to do.
"Mrs. Tempest."

Tad nodded. "That was ma-ma's"—he pronounced it
in the French way—"name be-fore—"

"Before what?" Ross snapped, forgetting to
enunciate.

"Before I changed it back to my own name of Peters."

Ross whirled around to look over the car. His first
sight of Sage was a shock. She was not her impeccably
groomed self. She had on a man's shirt, the tails
dangling down over scruffy jeans. She wore sneakers
but no socks in the August afternoon and her hair was
tied in a ponytail.

"Why?"

"Because I intend to file for adoption of Pip and Tad as a single parent. It's already in the works, and since my children are not considered class A adoptees, I think I'll succeed." Sage ambled around the car, her tall, supple body as graceful as always, her hand out to him. "How are you, Ross? And how's your family?"

Damn her! Who the devil did she think she was, being so cool with him? Hadn't they been married six years? She acted like a forty-eight-year-old woman with him, not twenty-five, more like his mother, not his wife. He had nine years on her to boot! Her slight smile and even slighter handshake irked him more than he had thought possible.

Sage stared at her soon-to-be-ex-husband, and was startled when her heart missed a beat. Those dark good looks that she had fallen for when she met him the year she was a senior at Sarah Lawrence still affected her as they had then. Ross was an anomaly! He had the swarthy skin of a pirate of the Spanish Main. He tanned at the first hint of sunlight, yet his hair was streaky dark blond and his eyes were jade green. He was very tall, a hair over six feet four, but since she was five feet nine inches herself, she had always been very comfortable with him.

"And you didn't think this was an idea we should have discussed together?" Ross had turned just a bit so that neither the boy nor the girl could see his mouth as he spoke to his wife.

Sage lifted her chin. "You can speak in front of Tad and Pip. They know all about you . . . and about the divorce too."

"That's more than I do." Ross spat the words, leaning toward her, his temper coming back in a rush.

Sage looked at him coolly. "You received your notification from my lawyer—"

"I was served in the conference room in front of the

board." He bared his teeth when he saw her lips twitch. "It wasn't funny."

"However did they get by old Beezenbuch?" Sage referred to the fortyish harridan who guarded Ross's office like the griffins watched the ancient tombs. Miss Beezenbuch had worked for his father and was fanatically devoted to the Tempest family.

"Who knows?" Ross cast that question aside, wanting to lash out at her. He let his eyes rove over her from sneaker to tousled hairdo. "Do you think you have a prayer of getting these children if I fight you in court?" It gave him only an instant's gratification when she whitened.

"Why would you fight me? We haven't been on the same wavelength for a long time. Divorce was inevitable."

"I don't see it that way," he shot back, angry that she should voice a vague idea that had been gnawing at him since he had been served with the papers.

"You don't see anything you don't want to see," Sage riposted, stung and just a little shaken. It had never occurred to her that Ross would put up a barrier to the divorce. Over the past year she had convinced herself that Ross had tired of her.

"We had as good a marriage as many of our friends. I could see that."

"You saw nothing then. Our marriage was a fiasco." Her voice had risen. When she saw the dog get to his feet and begin to growl, and Tad approach her and put his hand on her arm, she forced herself to be calm. She patted the boy and offered her hand to the girl, who ran to her and put her arms around Sage. Sage swallowed and looked Ross in the eye, smothering the jolt she felt in her chest. "I want more than the fairy-tale existence that I lived on Long Island. I want these children and the life we will carve out for ourselves here. I'm sure you would agree this"—she nodded her head to encompass the woods, the animals, the brick ranch house with the two-car garage—"is a galaxy away from what you're used to. Let's face it, the gardener's cottage at Highgate isn't much smaller than my house here."

He could have throttled her right there for discarding their time together like so much froth. He took deep breaths, trying to stem the ballooning pain in his chest. Rage like molten lava flowed through his veins at the cavalier way she was trying to dispose of him. He'd be damned to the hottest hell before he'd let her do that. "Since you seem to have all the answers"—his voice was silky when he spoke—"perhaps I had better hang around here until you fill me in."

"You can't stay here." Sage gasped when his teeth flashed in menace, his eyes jade fire.

Then suddenly Ross's expression became bland. He hadn't been president of TempAir, TempMining, and the parent corporation, Temp, for seven years without learning a little bit about jousting for position. He was damned if he was going to let the bitch yank him around like some blasted puppet on a string. She wasn't calling all the shots! "Have you considered that, even though you have been returning your monthly checks from me, your aunt's bequest won't last forever?" he inquired smoothly, becoming angrier as he noted how she hugged the children and how they clung to her. What a familial picture, he raged silently, the three of them bastioned against him! It was like swallowing liquid nitrogen—his insides were freezing and burning at the same time!

"I don't use Aunt Elizabeth's money. That's kept in trust for the children and their education." Her chin lifted higher.

How ludicrous this scene was! Ross thought. Sage and her cohorts were like the Mad Hatter's army! The three of them clinging together, the dog on guard, and that foolish wild turkey strutting about as though he were the hired protector. "And may I ask how you intend to support the children?"

"Don't be a pompous ass, Ross. I'm not one of your minions."

"Damn you, Sage." Fury and surprise rippled through him. By sheer force of will he restrained himself. The quiet girl he'd married would never have said that. He wanted to shake her for speaking to him in that fashion. Ross tamped down the anger he was feeling, knowing that he would lose control of the situation if he allowed her to get under his skin. He ground his teeth together. And she had come damn close already! he reminded himself. He took a deep breath. "It would seem that neither of us knows the other as well as we thought." He glanced at the house. "How many bedrooms in the house?"

Sage blinked at him, surprised. "Four. Why?"

"Ah, good. One for me," Ross told her, facing her again. "I'll be staying for a while."

"Why?" Sage repeated.

Ross frowned at her. "When did you become such a churlish hostess?" He felt as though he'd exhaled smoke. "I'm sure you wouldn't be that way if Jorge were visiting. Or has he been here?"

Sage glared at him. "You're being insulting to me and to a friend."

Ross ignored her and looked at the house. "Nice style. It looks comfortable."

"This is a children's house. You'd hate the clutter and the noise."

"Don't try to smoke me, Sage."

Sage could feel her face reddening. "You are welcome to stay for dinner, of course . . . and you may even stay the night, though I must say, you might be more comfortable at a hotel. . . ."

"Thank you for your gracious invitation." Ross returned to his car and pressed the button on the dash that opened the trunk.

"Would you listen to me? Something you've never done," Sage fumed, disengaging herself from the boy and girl and coming up to him as he lifted his two suitcases from the car. "We won't be here after tomorrow. We're driving to the State Fair in Syracuse to see the horticulture exhibits. We've been told by friends who are already there that Tad's sunflowers have won a red ribbon."

The boy, who had been watching Sage closely, beamed and tugged at Ross's arm. "Mine . . . and . . . Greg's."

"Congratulations." Ross put down his bags and proffered his hand, which the boy eagerly snatched and pumped. "I'd like to see your sunflowers."

Tad grinned and nodded.

Sage saw the boy open his mouth and watched in horror.

"Come with . . . us," Tad invited.

She touched Tad's shirt to turn him to face her, so that he could read her lips. "Ah, no. I don't think Ross would like—"

Ross reached out and tapped the boy, regaining his attention. "I would love to accompany you tomorrow." His smile turned sardonic when he looked at Sage's irritated expression. "And I can see I've delighted you."

"You'll hate it," she said in a doomsday tone of voice.

"Perhaps not," Ross drawled, his eyes filled with glittering amusement.

When Sage felt a tug on her blouse, she looked down at Pip. "Are you hungry, darling?"

Pip nodded, her doe-eyed expression more pronounced as she looked from her mother to the stranger.

"Not to worry, love. Louise will be coming to stay with you and Tad while I'm at the Gasthaus, and you'll like that, won't you?" Sage had turned the child toward the house.

Pip nodded, her eyes sliding from her mother to the stranger, who was walking behind them carrying a suitcase in either hand. Tad walked next to him, carrying a smaller case.

"You seem to have overpacked for just a day," Sage said tartly, holding open the black wrought-iron screen door so that he could walk through. "As I recall, you didn't carry that much when we went to Europe."

"Are you referring to our honeymoon, Sage?" Ross whispered as he walked past her into the terrazzo-floored foyer. "As I remember, the last thing on my mind was clothes." He faced her, the suitcases still in his hands. "You were on my mind."

"And that was the last time I was," she shot back at him. It took all her mettle not to step back when his face turned putty-colored and his eyes filled with emerald fury.

The ensuing stillness brought the children's glances to the silent adults, the dog moving restlessly as though he, too, sensed the sulfuric anger between the man and woman.

"Where is the guest room?" Ross spoke first.

"I'll sho-ow you." Tad went ahead down the short hall that led to the bedroom wing of the house.

"Ross," Sage croaked out, then cleared her throat. "These children have had enough trouble on their plates. I won't let our differences add any more turmoil to their lives."

Ross didn't turn around when he answered her. "Fine with me."

Sage stood in the foyer, her arms around Pip, not able to stem the shivers that ran over her skin. "It will be fine, pumpkin. I won't let it be any other way," Sage murmured to the child, knowing that she understood when her thin arms tightened around her.

Two

Sage stood at the work island in the room that was now a family room and kitchen combined since she'd had a neighborhood handyman open up the old structure to make it one large room. Sage liked it that way. When she was cooking or cleaning up, she could monitor what the children watched on television. They had a closed-caption unit for Tad so that he could follow most of the programs she allowed them to watch.

She was preparing chicken salad for their dinner with a fresh fruit compote to start. She was very fussy about Pip's and Tad's nutrition and made sure that they had more than the daily requirement of vitamins and minerals in their diet. When they had first come to her from Family Services, they had been slightly undernourished, lonely, and withdrawn. She had only had them for two months when she had made the decision to adopt them. It had been a delight to her to watch them flower. She sighed, wishing for a moment that she could stay with the children and share their meal. But she would eat at the restaurant as she usually did. A thought intruded: What about Ross?

"Very nice." Ross's voice behind her made her start. "Sorry. I thought you heard me come in. Tad took me on a tour of the house. It's very nice, and well-built too."

"Thank you. We like it. I'm afraid you'll have to excuse me"—Sage shot a look at the wall clock in the kitchen—"but their baby-sitter will be here in less than an hour and I like to feed them first."

"Baby-sitter?"

"Yes, I work most evenings—"

"You work?" Ross's words were grated out. "You have plenty of money."

"I earn my own. I'm part owner of a German restaurant about a mile from here—"

"What? A German restaurant? You've skied the Tyrolean Alps. You attended school in Europe. I know you have friends in this area who are from Germany. That doesn't make you a *Deutsche Köchin.*" Peppery incredulity laced his voice.

"You listen to me!" Sage interrupted him, rounding the kitchen island where she had been spooning chicken salad onto crisp lettuce leaves. "You don't know anything about my culinary abilities, not really." She waved her long-handled wooden spoon. "The few dishes I prepared in Casa Tempest do not give you the picture. As a matter of fact I happen to make many of the sauces we use, and we have a full book of reservations almost every night."

"And when did you turn into such a tiger?" Ross said mildly, his smile twisting, his temper leaving him as he watched her blond hair crackling with good health and swinging on her shoulders. Her blue eyes glinted with determination. "I've seen more temper out of you this afternoon than I did in all the years we've been married."

His remark fired her blood. "You never knew me." She enunciated every syllable in dark tones. "You only saw the shadow me, the one who was amenable, who never demurred, who moved through the life of a Tempest matron like the automaton I was supposed to be."

"Don't lay a phony machismo label on me. I don't like it and I don't fit it," Ross roared back, rubbed raw by her remark. "I encouraged you to pursue your law studies and your cooking." How could she talk as though he hadn't cared about her? Hadn't he held and caressed her night after night? Their passion had been wildly mutual!

Sage stood her ground, alternately glaring at him, scanning the clock, and observing the children to see if they were watching her or the closed-caption television. "And don't you lecture me as though I'm some school-girl. I always hated that treatment—and now I won't tolerate it."

Ross was rocked to his shoes. He steeled himself to mask his stunned rage. She had hated the way he treated her! "Why wait until now to speak out? Why not say something then?"

"I would have if I could have had your concentration for more than five minutes. Let's face it, Ross, when it came to me, your attention span was zero." She inhaled, seeing his mouth slash downward. "And if you dare to say we communicated in bed, I'll—I'll slap your face."

"Try it."

Sage reeled back as though he'd fired a weapon rather than words at her.

"I was about to say that I never remember you telling me that you had something important to discuss with me," Ross added harshly.

Sage aimed for the jugular, wanting to hurt him as he

hurt her. "Ross, if I had said that I wanted to discuss our marriage, you damn well wouldn't have thought it was important, so why would I try?" Why hadn't he stayed away? She had become used to the dull gray pain of being without him.

"And I'm damn well saying that you don't know me either," he bellowed at her, his control slipping, something he hadn't experienced in years. He lifted his hands, feeling them curl into fists.

Sage stepped back. Her gaze slanted toward the family area of the kitchen and she saw Pip watching her. She knew the little girl could hear, even if her brother couldn't. Pip had been traumatized by her home environment, but she had all her faculties. Despite the fact that the doctors had told her the child might never speak, Sage was sure that someday Pip would use words.

She looked at Ross again, her gaze dropping to his flexing hands. Lowering her voice so that the child would be less likely to hear her, she glared at him. "Don't you dare try to hit me either. Midas would be in here in an instant."

"When have I ever hit you?" he asked, outraged.

Sage stared at him, then glanced away. "Never." She paused. "Surely you can see how far we've separated. There's just emptiness and turmoil ahead. I don't want to be married to you anymore."

He felt as though she'd stabbed him. "You certainly speak out now."

"I want my own real life here with the children, not some glitzy charade. Don't rain on my parade, Ross." The words she spoke were lacerating her, but she wouldn't call them back. "You know as well as I do that our marriage doesn't suit anyone in your family and it certainly doesn't suit either of us."

One body blow after another, he thought with vinegary humor. Damn her! He would not let her call the shots. "I see. So what you're saying is that we shouldn't be married any longer, because of the way *you* perceive our life to be. *My* stake in this is so minimal as to be of no account."

"Don't be an ass," she snapped at him.

She pierced his ego again, he thought in grim mirth. Years of running things in the business world and in his personal life had accustomed him to people looking up to him, seeking his advice. "Charming."

Sage licked her lips, feeling as though she were balancing on a high wire swaying over a chasm. "Of course your feelings come into this, but—"

"I'm delighted you concur. I'll be staying with you a while until I come to the same conclusion you have about our marriage. It only seems fair." He walked around her, past the central kitchen island.

She hauled in a shuddering breath, watching him as he went to sit on the couch near the children and gaze at the television. "You can stay overnight," she whispered to herself.

She looked down at the almond-colored tiles covering the work area and tried to recall the joy she had experienced when this room had been finished. The work island was her favorite area. It held a small vegetable sink, a Corning stove, and a large butcher-block cutting board. Overhead were the copper pots and pans that she used to experiment at home with the sauces they used at the Gasthaus, their German restaurant. She had become addicted to German cooking when she had been an exchange student in that country. It was there she had met her friend Gusti and his family. Not only had she kept in touch with him, but when his family decided to emigrate to America it was she who had told them about Rochester and its suburbs. They had chosen the area to live in and Sage had seen them every time she

had come to visit her aunt. She sighed. Not even thinking about Gusti Baumann and his family drove Ross
from her mind. She saw Ross laugh at the antics on the
screen, Pip's gaze going from him to the television in solemn assessment. The child had seated herself closer to
her brother. Tad eagerly included their guest in the
show, explaining in his rather loud, dissonant voice
what the cartoon characters were doing. Midas
thumped his tail in approval.

Sage closed her eyes for a moment. It was better to
think of the restaurant than to concentrate on how her
life would change even momentarily with Ross back in
it. She envisioned a topsy-turvy—No! Her mind
slammed shut before she allowed the full image to enter.
No way was she going to change. The children were just
starting to be free of nightmares. Their life wasn't fancy,
but it was full. She ran over her days in her mind and
nodded her head with conviction. She was going to keep
this family on track. She wasn't going to allow Ross to
change it. Since the children weren't in school, she usually took them with her to the restaurant in the early
morning, when she and Gusti would decide on the
menu and she would begin preparing the intricate
sauces for the day.

Of course there were many that could only be made
after the order was given, and for those she was generally on the premises to supervise the preparation. If not,
Oma, Gusti's grandmother, would take charge. It was a
challenging and rewarding life. If she sometimes wished
she could exchange her law degree for one in accounting, the thought was only fleeting. She had put her
degree to some use in going over the contracts and
leases they'd had to sign. Sage smiled to herself when
she thought of the Gasthaus. So many people had pre-
sumed they wouldn't make it because the restaurant

was off the beaten track near Lake Ontario, not centrally located in downtown Rochester.

And they had done well, Sage mused as she carried a tray with glasses of milk, dishes of chicken salad, and fruit compote to the round table in front of the glass-and-screen-walled area of the room. "Pip, tell Tad it's time to eat."

The little girl turned to look at her mother, solemn warmth in her eyes as she nodded. Then she jumped down from the couch, made a wide circle in front of Ross, taking hold of her brother's arm and pointing to the table.

"O-kay," Tad said in his unrhythmic tones, turning to Ross. "Eat with us," he told Ross with his usual ebullience.

Sage looked askance at her older child. Such was the nature of the boy that he would invite the world to his door and give away anything he had. It endeared him to her, but he often threw her off stride with his openhandedness. Now was one of those times, as Ross turned to look at her, his saturnine smile telling her he was very aware of her discomfort. "I could make you some chicken salad. Forgive me for not offering." As he cocked his head, saying nothing, yet keeping his eyes on her, her discomfort increased. "I . . . I could make fruit compote too."

"Frui-it," Tad said eagerly, pulling on Ross's sleeve.

"Thank you," Ross said mildly.

Ire rose in her, but she pressed her lips together, set down the tray, arranged the dishes, then without looking at Ross, she wheeled and went back to the work island. She saw Tad gesture to his sister to bow her head.

Ross hesitated a fraction in time, then folded his hands and he, too, bowed his head.

"Ble-ess this food," Tad said as he did before each meal.

Sage bowed her head as well. It touched her deeply that the children still remembered to say their prayers as their own mother had taught them to do before her death. It was when Pip and Tad had gone into foster homes that their horror had begun. They had been more neglected than mistreated, often forgotten by the people who saw them as another source of income, not as young children to be cherished. Sage struggled every day to cleanse them of the bitter memories that both children had. And she felt she was succeeding, however slowly.

She frowned as she arranged a tray of food for Ross. She wouldn't let him disturb the hard-won peace that the children enjoyed. She looked at the man she had loved too much and shook her head at the foolishness of young love. Never again would she marry, but that didn't matter. She was her own person, and the children brought all the love she needed into her life. Never again would she give over so much of herself to another person. She had held back nothing from Ross. He had become her all, and she had given all to him, until finally she realized that the person Sage Peters had practically disappeared into Ross . . . and that he took it for granted. Sage was finished with the kind of loving that had made her wonder and worry about everything . . . even about when the time would come that Ross would want to discard her. She had wanted him so much that she was sure she had begun to smother him. She felt that he was drawing away. That thought had begun to obsess her and it ultimately became the impetus for her to leave him.

Early in their relationship she was sure he loved her as much and in the same way she loved him. Gradually she had come to realize that if he did really love her, it was not the sort of love that she craved. She needed more. She'd had the absorbing career as a public defender and the delight of learning the art of cooking, but there was a gnawing need within her. She should have discussed it with Ross, but there had been a gulf widening between them. Sharing between them lessened. Ross's work absorbed him and she began to build a separate life. She took classes in English at the local college, she joined the Y and swam every day, while alternately smiling at and ignoring her mother-in-law's mild censure. The Tempests had their own pool and athletic equipment; if they wished to go out for exercise they went to the Broken Oak Club.

Ross had not tried to talk her into using his parents' pool, Sage recalled as she carried the tray to the table and set it in front of him. Oh no, to her he'd seemed relieved that she had ceased pestering him to do things with her.

"Thank you." Ross lifted her hand and kissed her little finger, nipping the skin with his teeth.

Sage jumped as though she had scalded herself, feeling her face flame.

"Don't make a fuss," Ross murmured smoothly, smiling at Pip, then Tad. "Do you want the children to think that giving affection is strange?"

"I give them a great deal of affection," Sage said through clenched teeth, wiping at her finger, annoyed by the response that had rushed through her system.

"I'm sure you do."

She gulped. His smile was the same as when she'd first met him: indolent lightning that rocked her.

He looked down at his plate, schooling his expression. If she wanted to play hardball with him, he thought, his lips pressed together, she would find out just what kind of adversary he could be. He had never questioned his feelings about Sage until she had left him eight months ago. He had always known he loved her, and that was that. They had had a very good sex life—until the last year or so, an errant voice, like a discordant note in a choir, jangled in his mind. He wasn't used to questioning either his motives or intentions. Introspection, though not alien to him, was not dominant in his personality. The fact that he was questioning himself added fuel to his already simmering temper. Damn her! She wasn't getting away with upsetting his life. He stabbed at a green grape in the fruit compote, then smiled a crocodile smile at Pip. His smile softened when he saw her draw back. She really was a pretty little thing and as taut as a guy wire. "It's very good," he said to the little girl, who didn't change expression, but instead picked up her fork and imitated his way of spearing a green grape. Ross felt a strange delight, as though he and Pip had just communicated volumes of words.

And she had made that compote, Sage fumed to herself, whirling away to stalk back to the food island and begin cleaning up, one eye on the clock. She was banging the stainless-steel mixing bowls she had used as she washed them, something she never did. She had always taken great care with her cooking utensils. Replacing expensive pots, pans, and cutlery would eat into the profits. She ruminated in dark humor at her pun. She continued what she was doing, up to her elbows in suds.

"He-re, Mama." Tad handed her his plate, then rushed back to clean the table. It was his turn tonight. Later he would go and play ball with his sister and the sitter. When he returned, Pip was at his heels with her plate and utensils.

"Thank you, darling." Sage leaned down and kissed the delicately made child on the cheek. She took every opportunity to hug and kiss both children, but especially Pip. Even if Pip never spoke again, she would know that she was loved.

"Do I get a kiss? I brought my plate." Ross leaned closer so that, when Sage straightened after kissing the child, their faces were mere centimeters apart, the soft savagery of his voice stinging her.

Sage steeled herself, looking into his eyes, opening her mouth to retort, when the doorbell rang. Breathing a sigh of relief, she looked away from him to press the red light on the television to get Tad's attention, but he had already seen the red light on the wall, and he and Pip were off and running toward the front door.

"Saved by the bell, darling. Don't count on it every time." Ross dropped his mouth to her cheek, letting his lips linger there. "Ummm, I like the new smell of you— soap, various herbs, and of course your own delightful body perfume . . ."

Sage pushed at him, rocking him back a little. She studied his face. Only her very intimate knowledge of him allowed her to see the hardness behind his twist of a smile. He was furious! It hit Sage like an avalanche! She had seen Ross angry, naturally. They were both somewhat temperamental, but since he had been made the director of Worldwide Temp Industries, he had developed a cool, cynical facade that didn't allow for too many displays of emotion. She couldn't recall the last time she had seen him in the grip of rage. He was nine-tenths there at the moment. "That's the sitter." She walked around him, wiping her hands on a terry-cloth towel she had taken from the rack next to the sink.

She stopped and smiled when she saw how Tad and Pip clustered around Laurie, and how relaxed the eighteen-year-old was with them. Sage knew she would miss her when the girl went off to college next week and could feel her brow furrowing as she thought of that. Laurie's mother might be able to watch the children once in a while, but she worked two days a week herself. She mentally shrugged the worry away, telling herself it would work out, but still she fretted about bringing an unknown quantity into the house to watch her children when she would be at the restaurant.

"Hi, Ms. Peters. Gosh, you'd better . . ." Laurie's voice trailed off as she looked over Sage's shoulder. "Hello," the girl said hesitantly.

Sage felt Ross at her back and watched as his arm stretched around her and toward Laurie.

"Hi, I'm Ross Tempest, Ms. Peter's husband."

"Ross," Sage hissed.

"Gosh, no kidding? I thought you were divorced."

"We will be."

"We're not."

Ross and Sage spoke at the same time.

When Sage glared at him, his smile widened, making her shiver.

"Oh," Laurie said, glancing from one to the other, openly curious.

"The children are fed and the dishes are done, Laurie. They want to watch a show on television tonight and, though it's later than their usual bedtime, I said they could."

Laurie nodded, her admiring gaze sliding toward Ross again. "Are you going to be here this evening, Mr. Tempest?"

"Ah . . . for a short time, just until the children are in bed. Then I'll be going out for a while." Ross inclined his head.

Sage could have sworn she heard Laurie sigh in disappointment before she followed the children toward the back of the house. She turned on Ross. "Now see here, that girl is only—" Words dribbled away as she watched his face shut down as though a steel curtain had been dropped.

"Were you about to suggest that I might be planning to seduce that girl?"

"No . . . yes . . . I . . ." Sage blurted, then, as she watched one of his eyebrows arch upward, she could feel herself blushing. "I'm sorry, I—"

"You damn well will be sorry, my sweet wife," Ross grated out before spinning on his heel and going back to the kitchen.

Three

Sage went through the motions of making the white sauce with a soupçon of herbs and lemon that was for the light-as-air *Forellen in Weisswein*, a specialty of the house. Each piece of boned trout was almost platter-size, and it was broiled so delicately that it melted at a touch of the lips.

She knew from experience that the stirring of the ingredients for the sauce was most important and it needed all her concentration. Yet time after time she had to pull her mind back to the work at hand, her errant thoughts wandering to Ross when she wasn't on guard. Sage had arrived at the restaurant almost two hours ago, but Ross's words still ran through her head: "You damn well will be sorry."

She took a stack of pewter plates from a warming oven built into one corner of the kitchen, arranging the fish and garnishes of lemon roses and parsley in an artistic way. She drizzled a bit more of the light sauce that showed traces of green and red pepper and finely chopped onion, over the fish, and the platters were ready.

Sage was reaching for the bell that would summon Rickard, Gusti's cousin and one of the waiters, when she felt the hand at her waist.

"Ummm, that smells wonderful." Ross kissed her neck, then came up close behind her so that their bodies were touching. "Go on with what you're doing. I don't like to interfere with an artist."

"Why are you here?"

"Why shouldn't I be? I wanted to see your restaurant."

Sage felt like telling him to move away from her but sensed he was waiting for just such a rebuff and held her tongue. She rearranged the sprigs of herbs and lemon roses on each plate. "There." She couldn't restrain a sigh of satisfaction as she took in the splendor of color, aroma, and eye appeal of the garnished food.

"You are very talented. We should have fired the cook back home, but then I would never have gone to the office," Ross said with a hard laugh.

"Oh? I wondered what it would have taken to entice you to stay at home." As soon as the acidic words were out of her mouth, she regretted them. She hated exposing feelings like that to Ross! It made her vulnerable.

A throb of volcanolike temper erupted through him and was almost impossible to contain.

Sage looked away from him as Rosemary, Gusti's wife, came running through the door, blowing upward to get the bangs off her forehead. "Goodness, what a crowd! It gets bigger every day. Are Rickard's *Forellen* ready?" She stopped short and looked quizzically at Ross.

He stepped forward. "I know you're busy so I'll be brief.

I'm Ross Tempest, Sage's husband and Tad and Pip's father."

Sage felt her mouth drop.

"Oh. How do you do," Rosemary said faintly, rolling her eyes at Sage in inquiry before lifting the tray loaded with the four entrées and whisking it out of the kitchen.

Sage turned to confront Ross. "You are not my husband and their father. I . . . I mean they aren't even *my* children."

"And yet, darling, they won't be if I choose to contest the divorce. The children will certainly be looked upon as bargaining points by the lawyers."

"No," Sage managed to say in a voice that was little more than a croak. "I don't want anything of yours. You can keep your money . . ."

"The money's yours as well."

". . . and the cars, the house, everything. I don't want any of it. I won't live—"

"Dammit! You are not the only person to consider." Ross leaned forward, menace in every line of his body. "I might want children at this time too."

"You're too busy," Sage whispered, taking a step back.

"Don't give me that crap. The last time we discussed having children we *both* said we wanted to wait a little longer. It wasn't a unilateral decision!"

Anger grew in Sage. "I decided now was the time for me."

"I see."

She watched fury distort his features and she swallowed. "It's foolish to discuss a *fait accompli*. I have the children . . . and . . . and I'm going to the State Fair tomorrow," she declared, as if the thoughts followed one another logically.

"So am I."

"No." Sage virtually yelped the word. "You'd hate it. We're staying overnight."

"Fine. It's a good drive from here. We'll talk on the way."

"There won't be room for you in my car." Sage was foundering, feeling out of breath and out of sync.

"We'll use the Eldorado. Plenty of room."

She grasped at straws. "I don't like fancy cars."

"That's cute," he drawled. "You drove a Maserati, darling. They don't come much fancier than that."

"That was another planet."

"Calling our marriage another planet?"

"Whatever." Her gaze slid around the room as though she were looking for an anchor, something familiar to cling to while she figured out her next move.

"Forget it, Sagacity my sweet." His tough tone of voice pierced her thoughts. "You are through with running."

"You don't orchestrate my life," she said in a raspy tone.

"You're not getting rid of me. I'm with you all the way."

"You'll hate the pigs," she babbled.

Hard amusement moved the planes of his face for a moment. "Pigs? It's not necessary to love them, is it?"

"Don't be so damned cynical. I don't like it."

"And I don't like the way you've judged me."

"We don't know each other anymore."

"After all these years of marriage?" Ross seemed to mull the question he voiced, his chuckle bullet-hard. "You have a mole under your right breast. You have a small scar on your bottom where you fell off a bike, the left cheek—"

"I didn't mean that," she fumed, hands on hips.

"You could be right. There might not be anything worth saving in our alliance." He saw the pained look flash across her face and felt a black satisfaction that he could land a verbal blow after all he'd taken from her.

It stunned him that he felt so raw, so defensive. He couldn't recall the last time anyone had put him off balance . . . much less his own wife. If she had been a man, he would have retaliated with his fists long before now. That rocked him. The last time he'd mixed it up with anyone had been in college when he was on the boxing team. As it was, he had a desire to smack her bottom red and he had never had those feelings about Sage. He always had wanted to cheirsh her, protect her, take away all her worries and cares. And she wanted to repay his cherishing by throwing him out like yesterday's newspaper. No way!

"You won't like all the stuff we have to take on our trip," Sage suggested, trying another tack.

"I'll survive. Perhaps I might improve things. You never could pack to go anywhere. You always wanted to take even the furniture with you."

Sage shot him an annoyed look. "I believe in being prepared."

"Prepared for what? An invasion?"

She drew herself to her full height, irritated that she wasn't eyeball-to-eyeball with him. "If you are referring to the ski trips, I might remind you that we needed the extra clothing."

"Napoleon attacked Russia with less."

"Oh? Were you there?"

"I'm nine years older than you, sweetheart. Did you forget?"

"Very funny," she snapped, sensing he was enjoying goading her.

He sniffed the air. "You wouldn't have any more of that 'speciality of the house' you were making before, would you? I'm afraid the salad and fruit didn't fill me up as they did Pip and Tad. By the way, I like the children very much."

Sage curtsied, batting her eyelashes. "How kind you are, noble sir."

"How would it be if I sat down in that chair"—he

pointed to a pine captain's chair against the wall, then turned back to fix her with a stiletto stare—"and took you over my knee and paddled the daylights out of you?"

"You don't hit women."

"Not up to this moment, no, but somehow I feel myself coming around to it."

Sage lifted her chin. "You always said that the male who struck a woman was no man."

"True . . . and I still believe it, but you would try the patience of a saint, wife."

"And you're no saint."

"How right you are," Ross whispered, his eyes running up and down her form. "If you read my mind at this moment, you may think me a devil."

"I do." Sage coughed to rid her voice of its quaver.

Ross continued to stare at her. "Love, I do believe you look as sexy in that coverall apron as you do in one of your filmy nighties."

Sage spun away from him, going over to the order window and checking to see that the basic cooks, Dolph and Alica, were keeping up with the orders. Still ignoring Ross she crossed to the section of the kitchen where the vegetables were prepared. "May I help anyone?"

"Me," the youngest of Gusti's cousins, Helga, bleated. "I have to make twenty salads and Oma has been in here twice, glaring at me."

Laughing, Sage joined the girl at the huge cutting board, knowing exactly how Oma would be: rapid Bayerisch, the low German spoken by Bavarians, issuing from her lips, gesticulating, her apron fairly crackling with starch and energy.

Ross had followed Sage to the corner of the kitchen, propping himself against the wall. "What can I do?" he asked.

"Gosh, who's he and why isn't he mine?" Helga whispered from the side of her mouth.

Sage felt a stab of anger, then it was gone. "That's Ross."

"Your husband?" Rosa gasped. "Gosh, you didn't tell me he was a blond god."

"He agrees with you," Sage muttered.

"I heard that, angel." Ross patted her on the rump, not too gently, then nipped at her neck with his sharp teeth. "You're so sweet," he crooned.

"Oh Lord, I'll die," Helga whimpered.

"Helga," Oma commanded from the doorway, letting the door to the dining room swing closed behind her. "The salads!"

"All ready, Oma," Sage answered, grinning at the older woman.

"Good." Oma nodded once, then opened the doors again, snapping her fingers at a grandson hovering nearby.

When the salads were placed on the tray balanced by Otto, Oma looked around the kitchen and fixed on Ross. "Who is he?" she demanded, one quivering finger pointing toward him.

"Sage's husband," Ross drawled, coming forward and bending at the waist, catching up Oma's hand and gently kissing her wrist. *"Grüss Gott, gnädige Frau."*

Sage ground her teeth as she saw Oma smile and pat his cheek sharply. Damn him! His German had always been good.

"I speak English," Oma simpered.

Ross rattled off a spate of Bayern and Oma answered, laughing.

"I wish he'd talk to me in any language," Helga murmured to Sage.

"You certainly don't want your hand kissed," Sage said tartly.

Helga sighed. "I think I do, Sage."

Sage marched across the room to the order window and scooped up tickets. "Here." She handed a few of the orders to Helga. "We're busy." When she heard Ross chuckle at her back, she didn't turn.

All at once the kitchen was abuzz with activity, people whirling in and out of the dining room.

Sage forgot about Ross, her hands flying as she put together ingredients for the specialties.

By the time the last customer was finished and the dining room closed, Sage was reeling with fatigue.

Gusti bounced into the kitchen, kissing his fingers. "What a night! We're a success, Sage." He grabbed Sage around the waist and whirled her around the kitchen while the rest of the Baumanns laughed.

"Wait." Sage was laughing and out of breath. "What about the bad nights when you've come in here and told me we're ruined?"

"Never." Gusti wiped away those nights with a flick of his wrist. Then he spied Ross. "Who is this?"

Sage opened her mouth to tell him, but Oma told him first in a flurry of German.

Ross shook hands with Gusti and the others he hadn't met previously.

"I'm eating," Helga announced. "Sage, could you make me a sauce for *Forellen,* please?"

Sage was about to nod, but Gusti glowered at his cousin. "She's tired. I will make you a sauce. Mr. Tempest, would you like to sample our specailty?"

"Yes."

Sage went to help Gusti anyway because it kept her out of Ross's way. In the end she and Gusti made enough *Forellen* for everyone and they all sat down in the coolness of the dining room with their entrées and bottles of crisp Riesling.

"Ummm." Ross kissed his fingers in imitation of Gusti when he finished. "That was wonderful."

Gusti instructed the three young cousins who generally locked up. His father offered to stay with them and oversee the closing.

"I can help," Sage began.

But the cousins waved her away and began their cheerful and very orderly wrapping up of the Gasthaus for the night.

"I'll follow you in my car," Ross said as she donned the light jacket she had carried with her to fend off the dampness of the summer night.

"Uh—" She was about to protest, but something in his face told her to say nothing. She nodded, then busied herself in saying good night to the others and getting her car keys from the bottom of her laden purse.

"That hasn't changed anyway," Ross said. "Your purse still looks like a waste can in a girl's dormitory."

Sage lifted her chin. "Amusing."

He led her to the Cherokee and helped her up into the seat. "Quite a vehicle. I'll spell you on the driving tomorrow."

Sage looked at him as he leaned on the door, the height of him making their eyes even. "I do the driving—"

"Fine." Ross shrugged, starting to walk away. Then he looked back at her. "But I'll still spell you." His hard gaze took note of the frozen anger on her face.

Irked, she jammed the choke, started the car, then stalled it, put it in neutral, then started it again, forgot to keep her foot on the clutch, her anger increasing when the car leaped forward and stalled again. It was a matter of pride with her to drive a car with a stick shift, if only to sidestep her sisters-in-law and her mother-in-law, who always drove automatics when they weren't chauffeured. She could still recall how Ross had tried to dissuade her, but then when she was adamant, had willingly taught her on his Porsche, then bought her a Maserati of her own when he felt she had mastered the stick shift. She fumed as she watched the smoothly idling Eldorado draw up alongside her. Then she jammed her foot on the clutch and turned the key with a vicious twist.

"Flooded?" Ross leaned his head out the window and smiled up at her.

"Maybe," she grated, turning off the engine and sitting there with her fingers twisting together in her lap. After a few minutes she took a deep breath, not even glancing toward the Cadillac idling next to her, turned the key, crossed her fingers, then closed her eyes in thanksgiving when the engine turned over. Shifting out of neutral into reverse, she backed out of her spot carefully, aware that Ross was watching her. As she drove out of the parking lot onto the town road that would take her home, she was very conscious of the lights of the big car behind her. Trying to distract herself, she pushed in one of the cassettes from the small box she always carried in the car and wriggled back in her seat for the short ride home. She hummed along with Linda Ronstadt and tried not to think of Ross.

It had taken her a long time to get over missing Ross, but gradually she had come to accept that their marriage was over, especially as he had called her very few times. Ross! Why couldn't she concentrate on the lonely moments when she had felt shut out? Instead she recalled laughter, dancing, making love. She shook her head to clear it and sighed. The children had occupied her time and emotions, though. At a volunteer grandparents' program she'd heard about Tad and Pip from one of the other women. Immediately she had called the children's shelter and talked to the social worker. Three weeks after their conversation and after a thorough investigation of Sage and her home, Pip and Tad had moved in with her. Though the first few days were difficult as the three tried to adjust to one another, Sage recalled how each day seemed to get easier the longer the children were with her. It was then she had made up her mind to divorce Ross and put herself on the list of single-parent adopters. Very often at first she had spent sleepless nights wondering how she was going to explain about the children when the time came, but after a while she convinced herself that it wouldn't be necessary. They might even go through a divorce without Ross ever knowing she was trying to adopt the children.

Sage shuddered even now to think of how Ross's sisters would act if they ever met the children. Their high-powered personalities had been intimidating enough to her. "Because you didn't have the gumption to speak up to them." She spoke aloud. "And because you didn't want to share Ross with them, or anyone else." The vehicle jumped ahead when she trounced down on the accelerator out of emotion. She had never voiced that thought before but she shrugged at the truth of it. Maybe his sudden appearance in her life again acted like a truth serum, she mused in uneasy humor.

She had always liked her nieces and nephews, relating easily to their high spirits and often joining in their fun. It had been with her sisters-in-law and mother- and father-in-law that she had been the most uncomfortable. "If you had laid it on the line with them the way you do with Gusti when you have a disagreement, you might still be in your home on Long Island . . . but then you would never have met Tad and Pip."

She sighed, pulling away from a light and making a left turn into the area where her home was located. Through the open window of the Cherokee, she could hear the roar and slap of the waves on Lake Ontario as they struck the sandy beach. It was a comforting sound and one that she had loved since childhood.

Sage pressed the automatic door opener on the dashboard for the garage and drove in, sighing with tiredness and disquiet with herself for rehashing her life with Ross. Much that had happened to her marriage had begun with her. It had hurt to think that! But now she felt she had got on with her life and was doing well. She didn't want to do anything that could reverse or shatter what she had built up with the children, and she didn't want to think about the point of no return she had reached in her life with Ross. She put the car in neutral, pulled on the parking brake, and turned off the lights and ignition, then sat there with her arms on the steering wheel, staring into the blackness of the garage in front of her.

"Going to stay in there all night?"

Sage jumped and looked around at Ross, who was leaning on her door. "No. If you'll just move back . . ."

Ross opened the door for her, then, before she could get out, he put his hands at her waist and lifted her from the seat to stand her in front of him. He looked down at her, not able to see the expression on her face. "You're still very tiny." He squeezed at the softness in her middle.

"No. I work out. Muscular," she gasped.

"Ummm." Ross released her waist and let his hands feather up her arms, his fingers clenching gently on her flesh. "Lovely muscles. Hooray for working out."

"Yes." Sage gave stern, silent commands to her body when it wanted to sag against him. "Uhhh, I should get some sleep. I'm setting the alarm for six-thirty tomorrow."

Ross whistled, flashing a glance at the illuminated dial on his wrist as his hands rested on her upper arms. "That gives us just four and a half hours."

Summer moonlight slanted through the small garage window, giving her face a silvery glow when she nodded.

His lazy gaze fixed on her face again. Had she always had that fragile look about her? he wondered as he watched the play of emotions across her face. Bitter amusement laced his insides as he realized she was trying to think of a way to free herself from his hold. He could remember so clearly the days when they couldn't get enough of each other, how she had often followed him out to his car to say good-bye, how they would share lingering kisses one after another. He could recall the times when her kisses had wooed him back into the house again and he had called the office to say that he would be late . . . and in one case that he wouldn't be in at all that day. They had spent long, hot hours in bed making love. It still made him reel in sensual shock to picture how she had looked with one of his T-shirts on and nothing else, walking down the stairs with him to raid the refrigerator, then hurrying right back up to bed to roll and laugh and join together in the ultimate caress time and time again. Ross felt a shudder run through her. It irritated him when his body hardened in response. Before he could formulate rhyme or reason, he bent his head and took her mouth with his.

Sage couldn't stop her hands from coming up to clutch at his waist. She pulled her mouth back a fraction. "I don't want to—"

"I know," Ross grated, letting his lips cover hers again, his body shuddering with want. Anger and passion warred in him as he folded her even closer to him. How the hell could she retain such a hold on his emotions? His mouth ground savagely on hers as the amalgam of feeling tore through him. He heard her moan through the fever of his blood and he loosened his grip on her, but his mouth stayed locked to hers. He felt her body soften and meld into his and his breathing became more ragged, more out of sync. He let his mouth slide from hers and abrade her cheekbone. "You're still fire to me," he muttered hoarsely.

"Ross," she murmured, "let me go."

It took long moments for him to realize that she was indeed rejecting him with her voice even as her body and spirit embraced him. Fury tamped his ardor as he pulled back from her. "How do you manage it?" His voice tore at her.

"Manage what?" Sage fought to keep her voice even as she stepped back from him and rearranged her clothes.

"Refuse me while your body clamors for me."

"Don't be more of a fool than you can help."

"I'm not the fool," Ross said to her back as he watched her switch on the garage light, and open the door leading from the garage to the main hall. "I see that you have an alarm system, a watchdog, and a watch turkey. Cautious, aren't you?" He followed her into the house, while perspiration beaded his forehead. He felt as though some of his essence had burned away. He wanted nothing more . . . or less . . . than to take her to bed and make love to her until the sun rose.

"Hi," Laurie called, popping into the hall and smiling broadly at them. "The kids were great; went to bed on time and everything." The babysitter collected her things. "I'll be on my way." She winked at Sage. "You're a little bit later tonight than usual."

"Let me see you to your car," Sage said, but Ross harrumphed and peremptorily took over the task. When he returned, she kicked in the burglar alarm system, then turned to him, her expression grim. "Don't try anything with me again, Ross. We're getting a divorce and I don't want complications." And you can't stand having him hold and kiss you because you fall apart when he does, an errant voice deep inside told her.

"Saving yourself for someone else?" Anger laced his

voice at the thought of Sage manacled to a man, kissing him, digging her nails into his bare back. . . . He could feel his teeth grind together, visualizing it. "Has Jorge been here?"

"You're crazy. Jorge is married and, besides, I have no interest in any man nor any intention of marrying again." That was true, she thought sourly, unable to imagine anyone taking Ross's place.

"Noble of you."

Sage stepped back from him, feeling the heat and animosity he was throwing off. "Are you telling me that you've been faithful to me these past eight months?" She hated herself for asking the question. Ross had always been virile and very much aware of women, though she had been very sure he was faithful to her when they lived together as man and wife.

Ross could feel blood filling his face. "You left my bed and home and you dare to ask such a question?"

"Consider it withdrawn." She tried to smother the images of him with other women.

"You left me," he said in a thunderously loud voice.

"And you assume it had to be because I was interested in another man," she shot back. "You'd never look to yourself."

Impotent fury made his jaw clamp shut. He knew she was flogging him with words. Lord, maybe it would be better for them to be apart! They tore each other to pieces!

"I'm going to bed." Sage spun on her heel, crashing headlong toward her room, cursing the weakness that made her eyes stream with tears.

She undressed, swiped at her teeth with a toothbrush and her face with a bit of cream, then crawled between the sheets to curl into the fetal position, positive that it would be like the first few months when she was here alone, without him, that she would lie awake watching the patterns of light on the ceiling and walls. Miraculously, she was asleep in an instant.

Ross punched the door to his bedroom shut, then slammed his fist into his open palm. His aroused body irritated him. He wanted her, but he could have slapped her too! Sleep would be a long time coming.

He slipped in between the cool sheets, sweet-smelling breezes coming through the open window from the heavily wooded area behind the house.

Sleep came to him like a heavy hand just before dawn.

There was thunder, then the house began to shake as though an earthquake were in progress. Ross blinked himself awake and realized that he wasn't in the midst of a tropical upheaval, but that Tad was rocking his bed and calling to him to get up.

"We are go-ing," the gleeful boy told him in his high-pitched monotone. "Hur-ry."

"Up and at'em." Ross jumped out of bed, then grabbed at his toga towel on a chair to wrap around himself when he saw Pip peeking around the door. "Come in, love. I'm going to take a shower and—"

Tad shook his head. "Make the bed." He pointed at the rumpled clothing. "Every-one makes his bed."

"Gotcha." Ross was all at once glad he had gone to the private boarding school in Scotland that not only insisted on bed making but corner turning as well. He was glad of the skill as he noted that both Pip and Tad watched him closely. "There. Done. Now I'll take my shower."

Tad nodded. Pip stared at Ross wide-eyed, her thumb in her mouth, most of her body hidden behind her brother's.

Without thinking, Ross patted Tad on the head, then bent down and kissed Pip on the cheek. It happened so fast that neither child reacted. Ross left the room as quickly as possible.

When he returned from his shower in the guest bathroom, the children were gone. He packed with a minimum of fuss, just taking his shaving things, a clean sport shirt, and jeans.

"Uh. . . ." Sage stood at the half-opened door of his room. "We—I have decided to stay at the cabin. . . ."

Ross threw details around in his head, computed, and came to a conclusion. "The cabin that your family owned on Cayuga Lake and that you used summers. It was part of the package when you inherited this house?"

Sage nodded. "It's nothing fancy . . . you might not like—"

"I'll chance it," Ross said coldly, wanting to hit out at her for intimating that he could rough it only in the Oak Bar at the Plaza Hotel.

"Suit yourself," she said tartly, and spun away from the door.

He added a swimsuit to the suitcase, along with dress slacks and shirt, and socks. Then he left the room, closing the door after him, and went to join the others, who were standing at the tailgate of the Cherokee. He watched as Sage and Tad approached a large cooler that he assumed contained food and drink. "Wait. I'll lift that. Just tell me where you want it."

Sage pointed to a corner at the back of the vehicle.

In short order everything was loaded. The dog had been taken to a neighbor's house earlier and now the children stood talking to Morris the turkey.

"What are they saying to him?"

"They're telling him good-bye," Sage answered, looking fleetingly over her shoulder at Ross. "They're convinced that he understands that he cannot come here for dinner and that he is to go to the neighbors until we return."

Ross chuckled. "Maybe he does understand them." He

watched the strutting bird dance around the children and then peck at their bare arms, not seeming to hurt them.

"He's a wily solitary boy, otherwise he couldn't have withstood the tough winter around here. His peers that were put into the park at the same time didn't survive. Morris is a very special bird."

"You seem to like him as much as the kids do."

Sage nodded. "He helped me to get over a great deal of the loneliness when I first arrived here in Irondequoit."

Ross felt a constricting pain in his chest

"I didn't know anyone," Sage continued, "but there was Morris coming up to the door every day and demanding attention and feed. He's particularly fond of sunflower seeds and a millet I found at the Genessee Co-op store."

"Lord! He has a menu." Ross laughed aloud. Pip turned their way at that moment and Ross was struck by the fact that even though she was unsmiling, she seemed relaxed and content.

Sage clapped her hands and gestured to Pip, who pulled on her brother's sleeve.

The two children scampered over to the car. The wild turkey gobbled gently for a moment, then turned and trotted at a rapid rate into the woods.

Ross went around to the passenger side of the car after letting both children into the back seat and seeing to it that they fastened their seat belts.

"Uh . . . would you like to drive? It's stick shift." Sage bit her lip, waiting for his stinging reply.

"Unless you'd mind, I'd like to drive."

Sage nodded, relieved that they hadn't argued again. It shook her when he came around and opened the passenger door for her, taking her arm and standing close to her while she stepped up the steep step and got into the cablike front seat. "Thank you," she whispered. She told herself not to be such a fool. Ross was always unfailingly polite with women . . . all women.

"This handles like a dream," Ross said when they were driving down the winding side roads that led to the main highway.

Sage was inordinately happy because of his words. Fool, she told herself, you act as though he had praised you. Still, she couldn't quite suppress the giddy feeling of happiness that pervaded her at being in the company of her husband and children in the confines of the car.

Tad kept up a running commentary in his high-pitched voice, describing everything he saw and how much fun he was going to have in Syracuse at the State Fair.

"They're great kids." Ross was amazed at how good it felt to be with them.

"Yes. They are." Pride filled Sage's voice.

"I think this trip is going to be very interesting." Ross shot a look at her, pleased when he saw the touch of pink in her cheeks.

She couldn't seem to stem the unsettling delight that raced through her, burying for a moment the voice that told her it wouldn't last.

Four

The drive east on Route 90, better known as the New York State Thruway, was wonderful in the sweet coolness of an August morning. They stopped for breakfast at a small café that Ross knew off the thruway in a small hamlet called Violet.

"Flower's Café in Violet!" Sage said as Ross came around to her side of the car and opened the door. "I don't believe it."

"You'll believe the coffee. Here we go." He reached in and clasped her around the waist, lifting her to the ground, his mouth moving featherlike across hers. "Umm. I have always adored the lovely odor of you."

Sage stood there, knowing her mouth was opening and closing like a fish's, unable to formulate the words to answer him. Her body felt as though it were freezing and boiling at the same time.

"All right, troops, let's go." Ross unhooked Tad and he

tumbled past him out of the car to jump up and down with excitement next to Sage. "Now, you, my sweet budgie," Ross whispered to the little girl, who stiffened when he first lifted her, her face unsmiling and emotionless. "Not to fret, love. I will never hurt you," he whispered into the fine silk of her hair as he hugged her once, then put her on her feet next to her brother. "Now both of you stay close to your mother and me when we cross the parking lot," he admonished them, then took a hand of each.

Sage had to laugh. "How in the world would they run anywhere with the grip you have on them?"

Ross didn't laugh back. "There are too many trucks that come in here to take chances," he retorted, then marched ahead with the children.

Sage stared after him, seeing another side to the many-faceted man whom she would be divorcing.

Ross looked over his shoulder. "Coming?"

"Yes." She hurried toward them, taking Pip's other hand when she reached them.

The restaurant was pristine, done in white, leaf green, and violet. They took a booth with high oak backs and paper placemats sprigged in violets in front of each place.

"Pan-cakes." Tad grinned from ear to ear. "Sausage . . . or-ange juice-s-s."

Pip nodded, not stiffening when Ross lifted her to put a youth chair under her.

"How about you, Sage? Oatmeal?"

"Do they have it? I mean, the real stuff, not instant?"

"They did when I used to stop here on my way to Greek Peak," Ross mused, picking up the clean menu and perusing it.

"I never knew that you skied around here. We always skied in Switzerland . . ." Her voice trailed off lamely.

Ross stared at her, then nodded. "I agree. We didn't talk enough."

"I didn't say that."

"You were thinking it." He went back to studying the menu. "Yes, here it is." He put down the foot-long card and smiled at the young woman who stood next to their table, her violet-colored dress and apron starchy clean, her blond hair frothy with perm.

Look at that cinema king grin, Sage thought, itching with irritation. He'll have that bowl-'em-over charm when he's ninety. She had an urge to squirt ketchup down the front of his Brooks Brothers T-shirt.

"Sage? You do want oatmeal?" Ross was staring at her, amusement lacing his voice. "Will I have to feed it to you, darling?"

"Tha-t's fun-ny." Tad read Ross's lips and guffawed, turning some of the heads at the breakfast bar where some truckers were eating. Many smiled at the ebullient boy.

Sage felt a surge of irritation at both the boy and Ross. She nodded curtly at the girl, who didn't notice because she was looking at Ross. "Yes." She spoke to the waitress, and the girl's head turned reluctantly toward her. "I'll have the oatmeal, tomato juice, and coffee."

"Ah, right." The girl punched at her pad with her pencil, gave Ross one last long look, and meandered back to the short-order station.

Ross raised one eyebrow at Sage. "Tummy upset?"

"Don't be ridiculous," she snapped.

Pip sensed her mother's anger and slipped her tiny hand into Sage's, staring at her.

"It's all right, darling. Mother is fine. We are going to have such a good time at the fair."

Pip nodded, inhaling a shuddering breath.

Tad started to chatter and point at things out the window. Pip followed his gaze, listening to him.

"Sometime you must tell me what happened to them." Ross spoke in a low voice leaning over the table, so that his mouth was close to Sage's ear.

"I will." Her glance slid toward the little girl sitting next to her. "Her hearing is acute."

"So I've noticed." Ross grinned at her again, his eyes running over her face as though he were searching for something.

"Uh . . . how is everyone at home?" She tried desperately to get his attention away from the intense study of her features.

"Fine. Griffiths are getting a divorce. Manleys are getting married," Ross said, his eyes still lazily drifting over her features. "You have wonderful skin."

"Griffiths are a surprise," she said in a choking voice. She shot a look at the children, but they were still absorbed in the passing traffic and a big crow that was clambering on the top of a power pole. "Manleys are a shock. They lived together for over five years. I'm surprised they've decided to marry."

"Gil says that's what makes them sure it will work. If they hadn't lived together, they might not have been able to iron out all the kinks in their relationship. Now they believe that they'll be married forever . . . the way it's supposed to be."

"But you don't accept that?"

Ross shrugged. "If it works for them—"

"I think it's a good idea."

"You think people should live together in order to give their marriage the best chance?" Ross asked softly.

Sage bit her lip, feeling her brow crease, then she nodded. "I can't say I always thought so, but I do now. After all, most marriages have no plan at all. There should be a discovery period—"

"Apple pancakes, blueberry pancakes." The waitress leaned between Ross and Sage and plunked down the plates in front of Tad and Pip. "Two orange juices and two milks." She placed these in front of the children, her body effectively barring conversation between the two adults.

Sage fumbled in her purse for a moment as the children picked up their juice glasses. "Wait," she said to Pip, then handed the children their vitamins.

Without questioning, Tad and Pip took the three tablets one at a time, popped them in their mouth and swallowed them with juice.

"Vitamins? I didn't think you believed in things like that."

"When the children came to me, they were undernourished. They are eating nutritious meals now, but they still need supplements. Here, have some." Sage poured out tablets from the different bottles she carried, put three in front of her and gave three to Ross. She was nonplussed when he took his without comment.

They began to eat and Sage found she was very hungry. She gave Pip a spoonful of her oatmeal. The child took it dutifully. Sage wasn't sure if Pip liked it, but she had gotten into the habit of letting the little girl taste what she was eating. In the beginning, Pip had been afraid to eat her own food. The social worker had told her that often her hand had been burned if she hadn't eaten the way the foster parent approved. Tad had had no such bad experiences with foster parents, except that he had been separated from his sister. In the early months, the only way that Pip would eat was for Sage to feed her from her own plate. Though now the child ate alone and unaided, Sage still would take her teaspoon and give her some of her food. It seemed to soothe the child.

Ross watched and saw the infinitesimal relaxing of the little girl after she was fed food from Sage's plate. What the hell had been done to the baby? he mused grimly. She was no bigger than a minute and he didn't have to be a specialist to know that the child was too small for her age. When she looked his way, sensing his scrutiny, he smiled at her. *Someday, my little girl, you're going to smile back at me,* he told himself. Already he felt an affection for both children, and he was sure that he wanted to be in their lives. He was damned sure he wasn't going to be pushed out of Sage's until he knew without a doubt that their marriage was unworkable.

The children finished first and then had to go to the bathroom. Despite the relaxed atmosphere of the place, Sage frowned.

"I'll take Tad. You take Pip," Ross whispered to her, pushing his plate aside. "Then we'll come back and have another cup of coffee."

Sag nodded, relieved. She tried not to allow all the stories she'd heard about kidnapped children bog her down, but she took every precaution with them anyway.

"Ma-chine," Tad told her when she brought Pip back to the table where he and Ross were already seated.

"There's a bowling machine at the far end of the diner. I can watch them from here if you don't mind them playing. I've given Tad the money, but he told me he had to wait until you returned so that he could ask you."

Sage nodded and kissed the boy on the cheek. "Fine, but take care of Pip."

"Yes," Tad shouted, grinning, then he grasped his sister by the hand and tugged her along with him.

"They're very close, aren't they?"

"Yes." Sage turned to watch the progress of the children. "When I told Tad that I was going to adopt his sister, too, he cried and cried." Sage's voice shook. "Big rolling tears that I thought would never stop. Lord, they were so hurt."

Ross lifted her hand to his mouth for a moment,

bringing her head up. "And you hurt for them, didn't you, Mrs. Tempest?"

"Peters," Sage said hesitantly. "I'm going to use my—"

"You've made that clear," Ross said abruptly. "But you're not divorced yet." He drummed his fingers on the table. "You said the Manleys had a good idea—living together, that is."

Surprised, Sage nodded. "Not for everybody, maybe, but yes, I think it's a good idea for them."

"For us?"

Sage's mouth dropped open.

"Close your mouth. You'll catch flies."

"Insanity." She gulped. "We're getting divorced." Her gaze shot round the diner as though she might find the answer to her problem on the violet-hued wallpaper. "Besides, married people don't live together—what I mean is—" She fumed, staring at him as her tongue clove to the roof of her mouth.

"Yes?" Ross patted her hand. "Calm down. Of course a married couple lives together."

"I didn't mean that and you know it," she yelped, then lowered her voice as the counter waitress leaned around a customer to stare at them. "It's ridiculous," she hissed at him, keeping one eye on the row of people at the counter, who seemed to be watching them. "We've lived together and it didn't work. We're different."

"*Vive la différence,*" Ross drawled. He kissed her fingers one by one, seeming oblivious to the stares from the other patrons. "You have beautiful hands, darling, but they are redder than they should be."

Sage jerked her hand free, feeling embarrassment and hurt that he mentioned her work-roughened skin. "Work will do that," she snapped.

"Your eyes are wonderful too. You're as lovely now as you were when we first met."

He's spoofing you, a voice deep inside told her. Tell

him to try someone else, that you don't buy it, she was urged by the voice of reason. But nonetheless she sat there, entranced by his words, allowing herself to be caught up in his web. She had to fight her way out of it, not enmesh herself in new pain, be sick with love. She could recall when they first met. She had been an intern at his lawyer's office in New York City. That was how she was spending the last semester of college. She had already appplied and been accepted at Columbia Law School. She didn't want to think of those times, but her mind catapulted her back anyway.

She had come hustling into Mr. Howden's secretary's office, staggering under the weight of the law books she was carting to her small desk in the corner. When the door of the inner office opened and Mr. Howden had plowed into her, the books had flown from her arms to crash to the floor. All her stammered apologies hadn't wiped the frown from Mr. Howden's face, even when his client had knelt down on the floor and lifted the heaviest of the books for her.

"Just tell me where to put them, little beauty," he had told her when she had held out her arms for the tomes. Then he had followed her to her desk. "See you later," he said, his gaze running over her. Then he returned to Mr. Howden's side, saying something to him.

Sage had been sure it had been Ross's intervention that had saved her from a dressing down that day, but when she saw Ross standing next to his Ferrari in a no-parking zone at quitting time, she was going to walk on by without saying anything because she never thought he had been waiting for her.

"Whoa. This way." He had taken her arm and led her to the car just as a mounted patrolman had approached the vehicle. "We had better get out of here." He had grinned at her. "You blush very prettily too."

"Don't make fun of me." Sage had sat straight up in her seat, straining against the seat belt.

"I think I'm making fun of me," Ross had explained, giving a half laugh. "I had no intention of falling in love with a law intern today."

Sage could still remember how she had followed him dazedly when he had opened his car door to let her out, how she had agreed that they should dine together, how he had waited in her tiny studio apartment while she dressed in the bathroom. They hadn't come home until dawn. The next night he had taken her out again, and proposed to her. She had accepted and they were married in two months. She had continued with law school after marriage and passed the bar, even practicing as a public defender for a time, but nothing took precedence over being Ross's wife. And it had been wonderful! she reminded an inner voice that scoffed at her foolishness, that told her not to succumb again.

"It isn't too flattering when my wife daydreams when we are having a very important conversation," Ross told her, nipping her little finger hard with his teeth.

"I can't—can't—Before, you came first in all my dreams, but now it's the children."

Blood rose to his face. "I was aware that you sacrificed a good deal for me when we married. Going to school, managing my home, entertaining my friends. I was selfish and should have taken a deeper interest in your law work, and your culinary studies." A muscle moved in his jaw. "We both have to make adjustments."

"I'm making a life for the children and myself. I like cooking. The restaurant is doing well—"

"I could try moving my business from New York to Rochester to see how that would work. I can fly in to the Manhattan office once a week—"

"We didn't talk—" Sage whispered, panicky because she was beginning to think his plan might work.

"But I never said that I didn't like children. If our own child was born with a handicap, do you think I would have loved it less?"

"No." Sage knew that Ross was not repelled by any handicap, that his family had worked with the disadvantaged. His grandmother had singlehandedly fed thousands of families during the Great Depression and provided jobs for many more. The Tempests spoke with pride of Grandmother Ariadne Tempest, who almost had beggared the family with her philanthropies. All the Tempests were bigger than life! Sage thought. She had never fitted in with the Golden Era family that was the talk of much of the country when they went skiing in Switzerland or white-water rafting on the Colorado River.

"I want to try to mend our marriage, Sage. If it must be thrown away and destroyed, let it be because we couldn't fix the hurts, not because we didn't try." Ross leaned back against the banquette.

Sage fired one salvo of arguments after another to herself, but she couldn't find any argument that offered a viable alternative to his idea. She nodded once, and caught her breath at the warmth of his smile. "Does—does this mean that we'll—I suppose that we'll—what I mean is—" What was the matter with her mouth? Why couldn't it form the words into a sentence?

"We'll be sharing a bed. People who live together do that. That's one of the tests of compatibility we'll be using." Ross told her blandly.

"Don't rush me," Sage burst out.

"I'm not. I'm only listing all the reasonable things we should try before discarding our marriage. I'm being sensible."

"I have to think about it." Sage gazed at him warily. "You have a gleam in your eye."

"It's the sun." He pointed to the window. Then he rose

to his feet. "I'll get the children and we'll get going. You said that Tad wanted to see his exhibit before noon?"

"Ah . . . yes," Sage answered, but he was already moving away from her to the back of the diner, where the children were playing with the bowling machine. "He euchred me, outmaneuvered, and outgunned me," she mumbled, "and I don't know how he did it." She sipped the tepid coffee in front of her. "I should take a shuttle bus to Mars. He's probably planning to liquidate me with some kind of death ray. Oh Lord, I sound like a Saturday-morning cartoon. Damn him, he mixes me up."

He returned with both children in tow, his eyes glittering at her. "Children, don't stare at Mommy when she talks to herself. She's just a little harried. She can rest in the car," Ross said conversationally after tapping Tad on the shoulder so he could read his lips.

Then both children looked back at Sage, nodded, and moved toward the counter, where Ross was paying the bill.

"Am not."

"You say something, lady?" a burly trucker asked her as he swung his heavy body onto one of the swivel stools in front of the short-order counter.

Sage smiled weakly. "Talking to myself."

"Give up the coffee, lady. It'll help your nerves." Shaking his head he picked up the menu in front of him.

"Wiseacre," she muttered as she slid out of the booth and walked down the aisle to where the three members of her family waited.

"Ready, darling?" Ross crooned.

"Stop that."

"Mom-my . . . ?" Tad looked at her puzzled.

She could tell he had picked up her mood, so she gave him a reassuring smile before glancing at the somber Pip. She picked the child up in her arms and hugged her. "We should hurry so that we can see the exhibits. Then we'll go and see if we can watch the pigs being fed."

Tad forgot his uncertainty when he read the words on her lips and jumped to the door of the diner to open it.

Ross took the boy's arm and turned him toward him. "Don't run out into the parking lot. It's dangerous."

Tad nodded, his eyes glinting with excitement, but he stayed close to Ross.

"Let me take her," he told Sage, lifting Pip out of her arms, kissing the child and carrying her cradled high on his chest.

Sage took Tad's hand and followed. Anyone looking at them would think they really were a family, Sage thought, her heart missing a beat.

The rest of the ride, the children played with the games that they had with them.

Syracuse near the fair grounds was a madhouse. Ross had to park almost a mile from the entrance, but the children didn't seem to mind.

It took all Sage's efforts to restrain the enthusiastic Tad, who was literally jumping up and down with delight.

Ross took one look at the harried Sage and took hold of Tad's shoulders so that the boy faced him. "Mummy will worry if you dash around. I want you to stay near us and we'll look at everything."

Tad nodded, going at once to Sage's side and taking her hand.

Sage smiled at Ross. "Thanks. He's such a dynamo when he gets excited."

"Boys are like that. I can remember bounding up and down the stairs at Highgate and my mother standing in the hall with her hands over her ears."

"You were a hellion by all accounts."

Ross grimaced and nodded.

"Aren't you the one who put the dean's wife's wig on

top of the flagpole on Parents' Weekend and the poor dear had to go around with a kerchief on her head because they couldn't get it down?"

"I think it's still there." Ross chuckled. "My father had to do some fast talking to keep me from being expelled."

"Money under the table, I'll bet."

Ross nodded. "My father wanted to disown me. My mother convinced him that it would be better not to, so they could keep an eye on me."

Sage laughed aloud, picturing her diminutive mother-in-law trying to restrain her tall, strong husband from mangling his heir.

"Life is never easy for the rebel." Ross felt his heart beat out of rhythm when she laughed, his eyes narrowing when a jeans-clad young man looked around, his eyes assessing Sage's curves. Ross felt an almost irresistible urge to break every bone in his handsome young body.

Pip held back when she saw the rivers of people moving in and out of the turnstiles leading to the grounds.

Ross took one look and scooped her up in his arms.

Sage felt her throat sting when she saw the child grip Ross's neck. "You'll get tired carrying her."

He shook his head. "When she gets used to it, she might want to walk, but she weighs next to nothing."

Sage nodded. "And she's almost doubled her weight since she came to live with me."

"Damn," Ross said vehemently, his hold tightening on the child, his glance checking Tad.

They entered the grounds, where there were even larger groups of people milling around.

"Hey, lady, let's go. Tad tells me we have much to see," Ross prodded Sage, who stood stock-still. "Are you all right?" he asked, his eyes narrowed on her.

"Yes." She followed him blindly, clasping Tad's hand.

"To-oo tigh-t, Mom-my." Tad looked up at her, pulling at his hand.

"Oh, sorry, honey." She smiled down at the boy, determined to see today through his eyes and join in his enthusiasm.

The rest of the day was a blur as Tad dragged everyone from the horticulure exhibits, where his display was shared with his friend Greg, to the pigpens at feeding time.

"Look at Pip." Ross inclined his head to the little girl, whose eyes seemed to have doubled in size as she looked at the almost cow-sized creature who was the mother pig.

"She tip-ped ov-er her bab-ies," Tad caroled in his high-pitched voice. Then he laughed.

Sage leaned on top of the pen, holding the boy around the waist as they watched the antics of the piglets, who were the size of puppies, as they squealed and scampered around the huge mother. When an attendant brought a huge basin of feed and water and put it into the pen for the mother, she nosed her little ones aside. Two dared to get into her dish. She snorted angrily and lifted them bodily with her nose and tossed them into the corner.

"She's one tough mama." Ross chuckled, kissing Pip's cheek when she dug her hands into his neck in her excitement.

"Yes." Sage smiled at the little girl and patted her back.

"Bad," Pip said, and pointed at the mother pig.

Sage looked at Ross blindly. "Did she say that?" She gulped the question.

He nodded, cradling the little girl.

"Even the doctors weren't sure she would ever speak." Sage gave Ross a teary smile, reaching for the child. "Oh darling, darling Pip." She hugged her, wanting to melt when the child hugged her back.

The four stood there, wrapped in their own personal enchantment, in front of a pigpen at the New York State Fair.

"Shall we get something to eat? It's after one o'clock," Ross asked huskily.

Sage nodded, unable to speak.

They ate in one of the many tented areas where Italian sausage sandwiches were served, and though Sage frowned over the nutritional value of soft drinks, she gave in to Tad's pleadings to have them.

After that Ross took the children to the New York Indian exhibit, buying them both suede moccasins and turquoise-and-stone jewelry. It had become important to him to see them smile.

"You're spoiling them," Sage protested mildly as she saw how the children beamed.

"That's a father's prerogative." Ross held up his hand. "And please don't tell me I'm not their father. I am . . . or I will be."

"I was going to tell you that the Indian lady is waiting for her money." Sage chuckled when he spun around to soothe the scowling older woman.

"Look what I bought you." Ross held up a suede vest with intricate beading and design as they walked along the concourse. "It's too warm for today, but in the fall you can wear it when you do your gardening."

"Gardening? Certainly not. I'll wear it with my dress jeans." Sage smiled at him. "Thank you."

Ross leaned down and kissed her on the lips. "You're welcome."

The noisy furor, crowding, and shoving of the day took on a rosy hue for Sage. She quelled the voice that told her to beware.

At four in the afternoon both children were flagging.

Ross picked up Pip, who had been walking with Tad, and carried her to the exit and beyond to the large parking lot.

"I can wa-lk," Tad told Sage, smiling tiredly, but proudly. "I had fun."

Once in the car, both children curled up and were asleep in minutes.

Sage had Ross stop at a fruit-and-vegetable stand along the highway, and she bought peaches, pears, and plums, ears of corn and beefsteak tomatoes. "I brought some chicken breasts from home for grilling."

"You have enough food for a week in that cooler," Ross told her dryly, following her directions along the western shore of Cayuga Lake.

"This is a beautiful area," Ross told her when they pulled off on a secondary road, then followed a rutted driveway to a red-cedar-sided cabin sitting atop a cliff overlooking the lake. "You have a million-dollar view."

"And you'll get million-dollar cramps in your legs climbing up and down the many steps to the beach."

Tad woke as they were unloading the Cherokee. "Swim-ming." He and Pip scrambled out of the car.

"First we help," Sage told them, smiling when they nodded. She unlocked the cabin, first the door to the porch then the main door leading to the tiny but very modern, functional kitchen.

The children and Ross followed right behind her with the sleeping bags, the groceries, and the sundries they had brought with them for the four days they would be staying in the cottage. Tomorrow they would go back to the fair again, but Saturday and Sunday they would spend at the lake, swimming and lazing on the beach.

Ross stood in the middle of the great room that comprised the living room, kitchen, and dining area. "Nice." He looked up at the loft reached by a ladder, then walked over to the smaller bedroom, glanced in the tiny bathroom with a shower stall, tiny sink, and toilet, then walked to the opening leading to the bigger bedroom. "Ours?"

Sage swallowed, shaking her head. "I thought I'd put a cot in with—"

"Forget it. We're married," he snapped. "It shouldn't upset you to share a bed with your husband." He swung away from her and went out to the car again.

Sage's mouth opened and closed. She pressed one hand to her forehead. "It shouldn't, but it does."

When he came back into the cabin he ignored her, going right to Pip's bedroom with fresh bedding and a sleeping bag.

While she was putting away the food and starting the refrigerator, she heard him go up into the loft with Tad to make his bed, the boy chattering every minute. She banged her hand against the sink when she put the chicken breasts in a plastic basket to thaw. "Damn him."

"Swim-ming," Tad demanded, standing in front of her with his trunks on and his towel over his shoulder. Pip was next to him, her purple two-piece showing the roundness of her middle. She wore the pink terry-cloth jacket that Sage had made for her and carried her towel over her shoulder.

"I'll change right away. You and Pip can walk down to the overlook but you must wait there," Sage instructed, referring to the redwood deck that her aunt had had built out over the cliff that was seven wooden steps down from the top. It was equipped with foldaway chairs and tables for dining and a gas burner for grilling food, and the view from there was spectacular.

When Sage walked into the bedroom, Ross was already there, nude, just about to don the Riviera briefs he habitually wore. "This isn't Hawaii," Sage said, mentioning the hideaway they had on Maui, with its private beach where she and Ross had swum nude. She had always considered herself a good swimmer and had spent her summers in college as a lifeguard, but the first time she had seen Ross swim she had known she was no match for him. He had told her later that he had competed a few times in the triathlon, which meant he had to swim, bike, and run many, many miles without stopping.

"Pity," Ross drawled, staring back at her when she looked at him as though waiting for him to leave while she changed. "Here's your suit. I like the gold color with your hair and eyes."

Sage frowned at him for a moment, then shrugged. He wasn't going to leave. She took a deep breath, turned her back to him, removed her jeans and shirt, then her underthings, aware that his eyes never left her. Then she pulled on the gold-colored racing suit, cut high on the thighs, low in front and back. "Ready," she said breathily, turning to face him, biting her lip when she saw his obvious arousal.

"So am I, as you can see." He smiled that lazy smile at her. "But nonetheless we'll go swimming."

"As I recall, that used to cause you some discomfort," she said tartly, irritated with herself because she blushed.

"It still does, darling, but I can take the discomfort. After all, we haven't been together in almost a year."

"It hasn't been that long." Her shaking hand scooped up one of the clean towels from the cupboard outside the bathroom.

"It feels like ten years," he said at her back, nipping at her neck, which she had exposed by sweeping up her hair in a careless twist on top of her head. "I'm hungry . . . not for food, as you well know."

Sage almost ran out of the cabin and down the sloping front yard to the thinly wooded section of low-growing cedar that fronted the cliff. Ross's laugh trailed after her, twining round her and tightening like a silken rope.

Ross followed her down the stairway leading to the overlook. "Say, this is wonderful. You never told me much about this."

"I didn't think you'd be interested."

"You really think I wouldn't be interested in this? What a pompous ass I seem to you. Right?"

Sage opened her mouth to answer, struck dumb by the white lightning of anger in his eyes.

"Swim-ming," Tad sang out to them, tugging at Sage's hand.

Five

That evening after dining at the overlook on barbecued chicken breasts, baked potatoes, and sliced tomatoes and onions marinated in vinegar and oil, they returned to the beach, gathered together some driftwood, and made a bonfire.

"Toasting marshmallows is an art," Ross informed Pip solemnly.

She then turned and signed what he had said to her brother. As adept at reading lips as Tad was, he couldn't do it in semidarkness, and the flickering fire was little help.

Ross then peeled the slippery bark from two poplar branches and sharpened the ends with a small knife hanging from his key chain.

Sage pointed to the tiny implement. "I never thought it was a useful tool. I thought it was an ornament you carried—" She bit her lip. She hadn't meant to denigrate him by the remark. It had come out wrong. She froze as his mouth opened.

"It's a very useful tool." His eyes narrowed on her, taking note of the way she sighed with relief. Had she always been this defensive with him? So vulnerable? A resounding no came from deep inside him. They had been open and happy with one another . . . at first. He felt goosebumps of discomfort as he recalled how many times he had gone alone to the club when she said that she didn't want to go, how angry he had been the times that Sage had told him that she didn't fit in with the "club" people. He hadn't bothered to ask what it was she preferred. Guilt frissoned his spine. Yet when she had left him he had seen less and less of the club and the people they knew there. He had not seen it that way until now, but he had tired of the same boring round of parties and get-togethers. It had irked and stunned him when Sage left him, but at this moment he had to admit that not much of their life together had been geared to her wants and needs. He ground his teeth at the truth of that.

"Mo-re for Pip a-and me." Tad grinned at him and held out Pip's and his pointed sticks.

"Let's give Mommy one first," Ross said, laboriously trying to sign. Tad knew what he was saying before he finished and nodded.

"No." Sage laughed when Ross tried to feed her the brown-crusted marshmallow that oozed a hot, sticky interior. "Ohhh, you've gotten it all over—" She couldn't stop laughing as she brought her hand up to wipe her chin and mouth, relieved to think of anything but the night ahead.

"Wait. I'll get it for you." Ross leaned over her, his back blocking his movements from the children, as he licked her lips then pressed his tongue into her mouth. "There. Is that better?" She wouldn't meet his eyes. He

felt the tremor run over her skin and that angered him.
Damn you, Sage! He would never rape her, but he was
damn well going to sleep with her!

"Uh . . . yes," Sage gulped, a little out of breath, hearing the hot irony in his voice.

They ate a few more marshmallows, the children
seeming to enjoy the ritual of cooking them over the
flames as much as eating them.

It took Ross's breath away when Pip looked up at him,
her eyes soft, her mouth ringed in gooey marshmallow.
When she hitched closer to him on the blanket, he was
sure his heart flipped right over.

"It's a very warm night—what say we strip down the
kids and take them in the water to wash them off? You
take Pip and I'll take Tad. Don't forget to take off your
clothes. You might get them wet," he chided softly.

"I've been skinny-dipping since childhood, thank
you."

"Darling, what a delightful idea. We'll come down here
alone one evening and do it together." He remembered
Maui and how she looked, her golden body tossed on the
waves, her laughter filling the tropical night.

Sage felt strong and supple all at once, free and filled
with joie de vivre. She had forgotten how much fun Ross
could be. Suddenly she saw them together in her mind's
eye. The times they had sailed not far from their home
on Long Island, the surfing off the coast of Maui, the fun
they had had skiing. . . .

"Ready?" Ross came up behind her and lifted her into
his arms, carrying her out to the end of the dock, a
shouting and laughing Tad at their heels, Pip right
behind him.

"You wouldn't! I haven't removed all my clothes."

Ross immediately released her, forcing her to stand in
front of him as he removed her shorts and top. "Now
you're ready."

Sage braced herself to be thrown into the water. It shocked her when Ross jumped off the dock with her in his arms. "Fool." She surfaced in the shoulder-high water, coughing and laughing. She splashed at him as he turned and swam back to the end of the dock, and lifted his arms for Pip to jump.

The little girl hesitated for a moment then leaped forward, her arms outstretched to Ross.

Tad jumped by himself. Both children were good swimmers and used to deep water, but with only a slice of moon to tell where they were, both Sage and Ross stayed close to them.

In short order they were out on the beach again, wrapping the children in the voluminous towels they had brought.

Sage jumped when Ross came up to her and cocooned her in a fluffy towel. "That's the last one."

"Then we'll share it." He dried her quickly, took a swipe at himself, then wrapped them both in it. "Better?"

"Yes."

"I like it too. Look at those two, they're mesmerized by the flames. They'll be falling asleep in a minute." Ross finished drying her, then picked up her clothes and handed them to her.

Ross doused the fire, telling the children they would make another one soon.

By the time they had carried Pip and Tad up to the cabin they were almost sound asleep, so much so that Ross climbed up into the loft with Tad to make sure that he was tucked in and that the gate to the ladder was hooked shut.

He came down and looked in to see Sage tucking Pip into her sleeping bag. Then he went into the bigger bedroom to strip off his damp clothing.

Sage could hear him moving around in their—her

head snapped up in shock. She was already referring to it as "their" bedroom. The palms of her hands felt damp. A mixture of dread and anticipation frissoned her spine. How could she sleep with him again? It was insane! She shook her head to clear it. She was a fool to let herself get caught in a devil's bargain again. Marriage with Ross had been just that, she mused, placing the little girl's hand inside the sleeping bag, but keeping it unzipped because of the balminess of the night.

"Come out of there, Sage. Pip is alseep."

Sage jumped, his voice touching her skin like electric shocks. "I'm coming."

Ross waited for her in the large room, holding two tulip glasses and a bottle of champagne. "Found it in the cupboard. It's not too chilled. I only put it in the refrigerator just before we went down to the beach."

"It should be all right."

"I thought we'd drink to . . . life."

"Good toast." Sage coughed to clear her throat of its huskiness, and lifted her glass.

"Maybe even our life together," Ross said lazily, touching his glass to hers, and patting her on the back when she started coughing. He sipped, then smiled at her over the rim of the glass.

With an effort she stopped coughing and tasted the champagne, drinking slowly. "Went down the wrong way," she croaked out.

"That happens." He smiled at her. "We've had a big day. You're tired." He lifted the drink from her hand. "Come along, we'll finish the rest of this in bed."

Sage looked at him mutely.

"You know you have nothing to fear from me. I want happiness in my life too." He gestured with his head for her to precede him into the bedroom. "Happiness is only a minute, an hour, at most one day at a time," he whispered as he shut the door behind them.

She nodded, daring to face him and take the glass he offered, aware they had much to discuss, many things to settle, but consciously sweeping them aside in the warmth of the moment.

They undressed in silence. If she felt uncomfortable, she noticed no such feeling in him as he whistled softly.

He climbed into the bed, wincing as the mattress sagged toward the middle. He leaned on one elbow and watched her as she backed into bed. "You weren't this nervous on our wedding night." It rankled when he saw her naked back stiffen before she got under the covers, facing away from him.

"No." Sage recalled how eagerly she had thrown herself into his arms, welcoming his loving, reveling in the new experience, barely noticing the momentary discomfort because she was so caught up in the whirlpool of love.

"I have no intention of raping my wife," he said in her ear. "But you could turn around and kiss me good night, just like Tad or Pip?"

A shaky laugh bubbled out of her as she turned and lifted her face. They were nude but not touching. She kissed his cheek. "There. That's like Pip and Tad."

"Kiss me, Sage."

She turned her face so that their lips were touching, breath mixing, quickening. She rubbed her mouth against his, welcoming the magnetic abrasion.

His hands came up to grasp lightly at her waist, pulling her hips closer. "As you can feel I'm ready again."

"Yes," Sage gulped, giddy suddenly. His fingers kneaded her waist; there were taut vibrations coming off his body as he kept himself in control. She knew— even as she sensed the fever between them mounting— that if she asked him to do so, he would release her, however reluctantly.

The velvet indentation of her flesh under his hands

was erotic in the extreme. He could feel sweat begin to bead his upper lip. Silence stretched between them.

Sage sagged against him, wanting to hold all of him. Could she smell the smoke of the bridges she had burned behind her? The question dissipated in the smoky passion that enveloped her.

His arms closed around her and all his determination to remain steady fled when he felt her skin in a silky massage against him. Her lips trembled over his throat, feathering down to touch the flat nipples on his chest. "Sage . . ." he said breathily, his hands running up and down her body, feeling the spasmodic acceptance of him coming through her skin. He had forgotten the power she generated even before they had first made love. She put a match to his senses and he reeled with the hot intimacy of their union.

When he felt her lips part under his, her tongue coming to meet his like a gentle spear, all thought of teasing her for long moments were forgotten as he gave over his body and feeling to her.

Opening to him like a closed rosebud reacting to the sun, she felt all her tamped-down emotions rising like a flood and carrying her to Ross. She wanted to hold him and stroke him until the lava that bubbled in her veins overflowed and carried them both away.

"No, love, I won't let you hurry it," Ross drawled, turning her on her back, his words slightly slurred as he let his mouth slide down her body.

She thought she must have dreamed what she heard. Ross was not given to talking when they made love. She must have misheard him when he said that about entering every pore of her. Then her mind went blank and exploded as he entered her with his mouth in the most intimate way. "Rossss." Air escaped her lungs, leaving her helpless and thrashing on the brink. Every nerve end in her body extended itself to him as though she would be melted into him and become his other self. It was too late to say that she didn't want to remember the wonder of loving him. It was no use admitting that now, if they parted again, she would leave even more of herself behind. She couldn't go on without the life force that in essence belonged to Ross. All the long months when she had convinced herself that she could live without him were splintered in the moments that it took to join her with Ross.

Ross was awestruck as his breathing went out of sync, as his heartbeat lost tempo. She had always done this to him! Why had he allowed their paths to separate? How could she not know how important their life together was?

With gentle violence he brought her under his body and entered her, the rhythm they created lifting them out and up and around the orbit of the earth.

"Darling, you cried out. . . ." Ross soothed her shaken body, the love dew faintly salty and perfumed with the sweetness of her. "We have always made love beautifully, but this time it was so wonderful." He lifted her up onto his chest, so that her hair fell around them. "Now, tell me why you think we should be divorced?"

Sage stared down at him, dumbfounded, not able to form words, to clear her brain.

He shook her gently. "Tell me."

"I—I thought we were—so far apart that our marriage was just a document." She took a shuddering breath, feeling his chest vibrate underneath her. "I was fading into the wallpaper. I liked the public defender work I did. I enjoyed the work at the museum and the experimenting with recipes, but it frightened me that the only enjoyment I was getting out of life was in groups that never included you."

He had the urge to tighten his hands on her body, to squeeze the breath out of her. He wanted to shout at her to take the words back, even as he realized that she was right and that he had known it all along. "I wanted you with me. I asked you."

"Yes."

"Go on."

"But you never asked if I liked the company we were in, if I enjoyed the heavy drinking, the genteel gropings, if I thought it amusing that Hank Lemple came on to me after two martinis, that Syd Weidman suggested we could have a civilized affair." She coughed a laugh, putting her head on his chest, aware that his breathing had roughened. "I'm not sure I know what a civilized affair is."

"That's when two nations sit down and agree not to napalm one another," Ross said, darkly amused.

"I see. Somehow I thought it was more intimate than that."

"I will kill Syd Weidman the next time I see him." Ross said casually.

"Now, I know that isn't civilized." Sage lifted her head and looked into his eyes.

"We don't have to see people like that."

"How can we help it if—"

"We could live here, I mean in Irondequoit, for a while." He ran through his options. "I'll commute into the city on Tuesdays and come back on Thursday evenings. I can work at home the rest of the time." His nostrils flared. "We have to try to work on our lives together." It angered him when he saw skepticism flash in her eyes. "We'll putty the cracks, shore up the sags, buttress the weaknesses. We'll win."

Sage gasped and shook her head. "You can't work at home so much. You're the high priest of Temp throughout the world—"

"And I'll continue to be!" Ross's words were like hot coals tossed from hand to hand. "I like my work. It challenges me." He shrugged. "Barry is anxious to show his mettle as a vice president. He's canny and has common sense. I'll keep my hands on the reins, but he'll be doing more of the groundwork."

"Ruthless."

"Only when I have to be." He murmured the words into her ear as he pulled her down to him again. "I won't lose my business, but I won't lose my family, either, not without a fight. You and the children are my family." He kissed her hard. "We'll be taking many turns, down, up, and sideways, but we'll handle it."

Sage heard the rock-hard determination in his voice and suppressed a shudder. How could she have forgotten for a moment that Ross was always in charge of his destiny and that anyone in his orbit was controlled by him as well. "I—I won't give up the restaurant."

"I know that." He laughed softly, his hand stroking her spine. "You need me for that too. My German is much better than yours."

"So it is." Sage let her hands feather over his shoulder and neck, her index finger poking gently into his outer ear in suggestive rhythm.

"I like your finger spelling. The answer is yes, sweetheart. I would like to make love to you again." He flipped her over on her back. "I like the special code you used to ask me."

"You're too clever for your own good." She drew a long fingernail down his face, feeling charmed and irritated by the powerful man who was her husband.

"And you're very beautiful. Have I told you that I love women with long, shapely legs whose lovely forms sway in rhythm when they walk? Do you know that I love honey hair and skin that's pinkish cream-colored?"

Sage could feel her body heating from her toes to her throat. The words that poured out of Ross were delighting her. "I'll be very conceited." She laughed shakily, kissing the corner of his mouth. How could she be doing this when she had made up her mind never to see this man again? It was crazy . . . but so right!

"Your tender skin burns without sun screen but when you get that light golden glow you shoot my temperature right through the roof. Then you're my golden girl."

"Why have you never talked like this before?" She felt a sudden shyness, as though the man caressing her body were a stranger.

"I've been a fool with you. I took so much for granted. I always had the feeling you could read me so well that you knew what I was thinking about you. But also, I didn't want to be too intense with you. You were young." He kissed her cheek. "You must have known I was proud of you."

Sage nodded against his shoulder. "But I thought it was the kind of pride that said, Her slip isn't showing, she hasn't fallen face first into the soup, ergo, she doesn't disgrace me."

"Dammit, Sage." Ross's chest rumbled with the force of his words.

"Well, you never really said you loved me after our honeymoon." The words tumbled from her throat like thorns. She had never wanted him to know her hurt.

"Neither have you," he retorted quietly.

That rocked her! She had never considered that Ross wouldn't know she was totally committed to him from the moment she had cannoned into him in the law office that represented him.

"I think, maybe, we have to take a good, hard look at our life together, consider who we are and who we can be," Ross told her, his words muted against her skin. "We have to do better."

"And what if we find that we're not only not suited for marriage but not suited for each other?" The words tore from her throat. She felt a sudden upheaval in the chest under her cheek.

"That we handle on the day it happens. For now we forget it. I, for one, have enjoyed the last two days."

"Me too," Sage admitted, wary of giving too much away, desiring to hide a great deal from Ross.

"That's a start." He let his lips course down her cheek, nibbling as he went. "Did you want to talk about anything else?" His tongue touched her navel.

"Me?" Sage squeaked. "Heck no."

"Good." Ross gave a shaky chuckle, his face pressed to her lower abdomen. "You do have the sweetest, softest skin."

"I'm glad," Sage whispered.

The firestorm took them and thrust them out of the stratosphere, where the oxygen was in short supply, the giddy pressure of love popping their veins, joining their bodies and their arteries in a cumulative burst of sensuous love.

Sage slid against the moist warmth of him, her breathing still ragged, feeling the out-of-rhythm beats of his heart under her ear. "Wonderful," she mumbled.

Ross woke the next morning feeling at first the angst that had been a part of his wakening for many, many months. A warm weight on one side of his chest made him turn his head. He inhaled deeply as the gold hair sprayed over him, tickling his nose. He tightened his hands on Sage, kissing her hair, bringing his mouth close to hers, heat building in him at once.

"Hi-i Ro-ss." Tad beamed at him as he opened the door to their bedroom. "Mom-my is still sleeping?"

Ross stared at the boy, aware that his mouth was hanging open. He had forgotten all about Pip and Tad when he'd risen in the night to use the bathroom. He had returned to the bedroom without locking the door behind him. Now, as he looked at the grinning boy and the tiny solemn girl with her thumb in her mouth, he couldn't help but smile at them. So this is what his friends talked so much about—when they said there was no more privacy after children. Well, he would have to figure something out. He wanted to make love to Sage in the mornings as well as at night. "Hi. Hungry?"

The two nodded.

Ross was once more impressed with the way Tad could read lips. He knew some older people with decades of experience who couldn't do as well. Ross eased himself away from Sage, who grumbled in her sleep, then he put his index finger to his lips. "We'll let Mommy sleep. How does an omelet sound to you two?"

Tad nodded his head. Pip looked worried.

"Pi-ip likes oatmeal. I like om-me-let."

"Ah. Good. I think I can handle that. You get the dishes out and set the table on the porch." He had no intention of jumping out of bed naked in front of the children. They didn't know him that well and he wasn't going to do anything that might make them fearful. He would have to ask Sage about Pip's troubles in the foster homes, he decided, sliding out of the bed and pulling on his swimsuit and a pair of jogging shorts over it.

He went out into the main room and watched the children scurrying back and forth from the porch to the kitchen area, carrying dishes and silverware. They had even pushed over the step stool and retrieved the bowls from the high cupboards. He saw the cereal box and groaned inwardly. He could whisk eggs, but he wasn't sure about hot cereal. "Hey, who would like to go swimming before we eat?"

Tad nodded, one finger pressed over his lips to remind himself to be quiet. Pip had a happy glitter in her eyes, even though her facial expression hadn't changed.

"Get your suits, then." Ross smiled at the little girl before she scampered into her room and closed the door.

Tad was up the ladder and into the loft like a monkey.

In minutes they were all walking down the steep staircase leading to the beach.

Before Ross could even remove his jogging shorts, the two children had run out to the end of the dock and jumped into the water. Feeling an exuberance he hadn't felt in years, he watched them for a moment, then ran along the wooden dock with the boat hoist next to it and flung himself outward in a shallow dive that cleared him well into deeper water. He paced himself with the children and was both delighted and startled at the expert way they swam.

"We swi-im on a te-am," Tad told him, stroking next to Pip, breathing in proper rhythm.

"And you do well." Ross breaststroked next to them, loving the silky coolness of the lake water on his skin.

They swam and cavorted for about fifteen minutes. Then they dried off and began the steep climb back up the stairs to the cottage.

"Mom-my is tired," Tad told Ross as they approached the porch.

Ross could feel his facial muscles tighten. She *was* tired! He had seen that when he watched her working in the restaurant. Damn her! Why did she have to push herself that way? And he had added to it last night, he recalled ruefully, but he'd had to make love to her.

The children were surprisingly quiet and patient as Ross painstakingly followed the instructions on the round container of oatmeal. It pleased him when the little girl nodded and picked up the big spoon to eat her cereal and milk. Though there was no change of expression she seemed to enjoy her food.

When Tad jumped up and ran up the steps from the porch into the kitchen area for the napkins they had for-

gotten, Ross leaned across the table and touched Pip's
forehead. She looked up at him, a circle of milk on her
mouth, but she didn't flinch. "Do you think you'll ever
say any more words to us, Pippa? I hope you do, darling,
because I'm beginning to think you are the most beautiful little girl in the world."

Pip continued to watch him for a moment, then went
back to eating her oatmeal.

Ross sipped his coffee and watched Tad tear into his
omelet and munch his toast, feeling very contented.
"Look, there's an early water-skier out on the lake."

The children turned their heads.

"I did that on-ce," Tad told him, his eyes wide and
eager. "Mom-my says we'll buy a bo-at one day."

"Why don't we buy one today? I saw a place that sells
boats on the highway not far from here. We could stop
there on our way to the fair." Ross felt an alien excitement as the children's eyes widened in delight. When
they grinned like that he felt he could have bought them
the *Queen Mary*!

"Cou-ld we?"

Pip sat there, her spoon poised in midair until Ross
nodded.

"Could we what? And why didn't anyone wake me?"
Sage stood in the doorway leading to the great room,
smothering a yawn with her hand.

"We felt you needed your rest." Ross's gaze traveled
over her body, the cotton dressing gown not hiding her
curves. "I'm going to see to it that you don't get
overtired."

"Are you now!" Sage was both surprised and amused
at his grim tone. She felt her being suffuse with heat as
she thought of last night and their lovemaking.

"Mom-my, eat. Hur-ry," Tad told her.

Sage leaned over Pip and kissed Tad, then kissed Pip.
"Oh? Why should I hurry?"

"We're going to leave early for the fair, so that we can look at some boats." Ross fixed her with his eyes. If she made one remark about not being able to afford it, he was going to carry her down to that lake and dump her in it! He was damned if he was going to allow her to spoil the fun of giving something to the children! He wanted to do that more than he could ever say.

Sage opened her mouth, then closed it again. She looked everywhere but at Ross, sensing the electric charge of his temper barely on hold. "Who, ah, who made the oatmeal?"

"I did," Ross told her, grinning ruefully, relieved that she didn't put a damper on the boat buying. "I'm catching on fast to signing; Pip spelled to Tad that my oatmeal wasn't as good as yours."

Sage laughed. "But she ate it all."

"I think she was trying to spare my feelings."

"I'd like some."

"You would? I was just going to scrape it out on the lawn. Tad tells me you have a raccoon that eats everything."

"Including the plastic junk bags I put out." Sage sighed when he chuckled. "I'm not sure if it's a group or just one, but the damage is something else unless I keep it in the shed until pickup morning."

Ross nodded and rose, going into the kitchen and heating up the cooling oatmeal by adding warm milk and putting it on to simmer.

Sage bit her lip when she looked at the soupy concoction Ross placed in front of her. She lifted her spoon and began to eat, aware that he never took his eyes from her face.

Later, they all took a swim, then dressed for the day at the fair.

"Are we coming back here tonight?" Ross said at her back as they walked up the slight incline from the cottage to the car, parked under some trees. He let his hand slide over her backside. "Ummm. Lovely curves."

"Stop that." Sage was more irritated with her body's response to him than she was with Ross. "Yes. Remember we said that we would, then go home Sunday afternoon? I have to work tomorrow night—"

"Can't you delegate more than you do? I think you're overworking."

Sage was about to disagree, then she shrugged. "I am, a little, but that's the price of owning a business, especially a restaurant."

"I want to go over the books and the ways and means with you. It might be cost effective to have another chef who brings along his own recipes. Might prevent the cooking from becoming hackneyed. Who knows? It might be innovative for the menu."

Sage got into the passenger seat, first checking to see that the children fastened their seat belts. "I hadn't thought of that. Won't that be a great deal of trouble for you, running a time study on us?"

Ross leaned across the front seat, letting his mouth run down her cheek. "It would be a pleasure just to make sure you had more time for me."

"Ross." She half-laughed, half-frowned, his hot, lazy gaze melting her bones.

"Are you happy? At this minute?" He put the car in gear and turned around on the expanse of backyard, then drove out the bumpy drive to the secondary road that horseshoed onto the highway.

Sage hardly had to think of her answer. "Yes, I'm happy." She didn't add that she wondered how long it would last.

"So am I. Let's not think beyond that. You'll have to admit that it's a good beginning."

"Yes." She didn't push his hand away when it came

over and covered her thigh, the heat from his hand penetrating the thin cotton of her slacks.

The Robin's Nest Marina was about ten miles from the cabin in the direction they would be taking to the fair.

"The new owners are former football players." Sage read the small biography in the window of the boat store. She showed Tad and Pip the pictures of the two men in their uniforms. She looked around at Ross as he ushered them in the door. "Do you think we'll be at the lake enough to justify a boat?" she asked, her Scottish forebears dictating her frugality.

"I think so. Let's look at them anyway." Ross helped her through the door, admonishing both children to stay at his side.

Sage gasped at the number and kinds of watercraft that Bubba Taylor and Grit Daystrom, the two former football players, had displayed.

The children were ecstatic at the choices and happily climbed up, or were hoisted up, into several of the sleek crafts.

"This is going to cost," Sage said from the side of her mouth as she moved up and down the converted barnlike structure.

"Don't twist your mouth that way, sweetheart. It will make your lips sore," Ross crooned, taking hold of her upper arms and shaking her gently. "It makes me very happy to see those two smile, not to mention what it does to me when you look that way."

Sage felt like a wet noodle when he leaned over and kissed her on the mouth right in front of the two owners, leviathans who were grinning openly. "The children," Sage murmured, whirling around and going back to where Pip and Tad were bouncing energetically on the stern seat of an inboard-outboard speedboat. "Come down from there."

Pip came at once, then turned and finger-spelled to

Tad, who had not been looking at his mother when she spoke.

"All-right." His high-pitched too-loud voice seemed to echo up into the rafters of the cavernous boathouse. He climbed down, then looked away from Sage. "Ro-oss." Tad pointed and scrambled down the narrow aisle, catapulting himself at Ross.

Sage watched as Ross scooped the boy up in his arms with a laugh. Tad looked surprised, but not displeased, as he studied the mouths of Ross and the two men.

Ross turned to Sage. "We bought the gold boat with the gold-flecked paint. I thought we could call the boat"—Ross hadn't released the boy, but he kept his eyes on Sage—"*Golden Girl.* What do you think?" He couldn't keep elation from his voice as he walked toward her. It was wonderful to buy things for his family!

Sage sagged against a navy blue speedboat as Ross set Tad on his feet, then at once lifted Pip.

"What does Daddy's girl think?" he cooed to the tiny child.

"Yes." Pip's positive response echoed up and around the building.

"Did she ta-lk?" The alert Tad pulled at Ross's sleeve.

"She said yes," Sage managed before going over and lifting Pip from Ross's arms and hugging the child, aware that the two burly owners of Robin's Nest Marina were puzzled.

"Our son is hearing impaired," Ross explained. "And up until a day ago, when she said her first word, our daughter has been mute."

"Oh." One of the big men reached out and touched Pip on the cheek, the other one ruffled Tad's hair.

"This calls for a celebration at the fair"—Ross turned to one of the men—"and I think you should include that Sunfish we looked at back there." He inclined his head to the back of the warehouse.

Sage gulped a laugh at her extravagant husband, seeing the sheen of tears in his eyes as he looked first at her and Pip, then clasped Tad's shoulder as the boy stood in front of him. "Are you going to buy the place?"

"Maybe." His voice was husky as he looked at her.

"We haven't a hoist big enough."

"Not to worry, ma'am, your husband already thought of that. Bubba and two of our men are going down to your property and install a larger one. You can use the smaller one for the sailboat."

Sage had to smile as she watched Ross sign something and hand Grit a gold credit card. He was flushed with excitement!

Back in the car, Tad chattered nonstop to his sister.

Ross put the car in gear and pulled onto the highway. "I don't think Pip's going to get to talk too much even when she decides she's ready."

Sage smiled. "They're both on cloud nine because of the boat." She swiveled to face him, her body straining against her seat belt. "But they're not any more delighted with it than you are."

Ross grinned sheepishly. "I haven't had this much fun in a long time. I think I could get addicted to the feeling." Ross challenged her with his eyes.

Six

They spent long, enjoyable hours at the fair again, then went back to the cottage for the night.

The boats were delivered the next day. Tad and Pip had almost as much fun watching the installation as they had riding in the new speedboat.

Ross was very cautious about the waterskiing with Tad and only allowed Pip to go with him on his shoulders when he skied.

That night the children fell asleep almost at once.

It was when they were almost home to Irondequoit the following day that Sage mentioned the boats again. "Ross." Sage hitched over to him. "About the boats."

"What about them?"

"They're nice but where will we store them? School begins after Labor Day and I usually close the cottage then too. Wasn't it a little extravagant to buy two boats at the end of the season?"

"Not at all. My friend Bubba informs me that boat prices will be much higher next season. Why don't we try to go to the lake on weekends when the children are in school? Then, at the end of September, we'll let Robin's Nest Marina store the boats until spring."

"Will you want to go to the lake every weekend?"

"Yes."

"Just like that?"

"Yes." Ross chuckled and put his arm around her, pulling her close to his side. "It will be fun. You'll see."

"But September will be busy at the restaurant. I'm not sure I can take every weekend off."

"We'll play it by ear. Whatever one we can take, we will. The rest of the time we'll work in the restaurant."

"We?"

"Yes. I have an itch to see my wife making *Kartoffel knödel*."

"I'm fairly good at it . . . but actually I'm better at the sauces."

"It makes me hungry to think about it."

An hour and a half after leaving the lake he turned in the driveway leading to Sage's house.

The children were yawning although it wasn't much past the middle of the day, the busy moments at the fair and on the lake catching up with them.

"Those two will want a nap, I think." Sage grinned at Ross, but her grin slipped from her face when he gazed at her speculatively. "What's on your mind?"

"I think we could use a nap as well. I have to call the office and my parents. . . ."

Sage gave him a searching glance. "Are you saying that you left town without telling anyone where you were going?"

"I would say that's an accurate statement. As you know, I have a very efficient staff and Barry would tell my parents I was out of town."

"Ross, you can't do that. The business!"

"The business is doing fine." He unloaded two of the big suitcases and carried them into the house, Sage trotting at his heels with two smaller ones.

They were still going one behind the other when they went out to the car again, Sage trying to get him to call his office at once.

Finally, after they had settled the children, Ross called his office. He talked for over an hour and it pleased him that his staff had handled things well. "Yes. I'll come in to work on Tuesday and Wednesday, but I'll be coming back here on Thursday," he told Barry, but didn't explain further. He hung up the phone, staring at it for long moments. Why hadn't he done this before, passed the mantle of authority to members of his personal staff and even his own family at different times during the year so that he and Sage could have been together more often?

He dialed his mother's home, glancing at his wrist-watch. His father and mother would be having a small glass of wine before they dined, nibbling on slices of apple and pear and cheese. He smiled when he thought of them. Neither ever diverted from the health regimen they had set themselves when his father had had a heart attack some ten years previously. Though the doctors pronounced his father's heart better than it had been even twenty years before, both parents would not change their healthy habits of walking every evening, swimming every morning, and filling their diet with nutritious fruits and vegetables.

"Sinjon, darling . . ." His mother's reedy voice came over the wire. "Stephens says you are with Sage." She referred to the butler who had been with them for over thirty years.

"Yes. We—she has two children she is adopting—wants to adopt—" He was irked with himself that he was foundering while explaining. "We have decided to live here for a while."

"Oh?" his mother said warily.

Ross could hear her whispering to his father. He braced himself.

"What the devil's going on, Sinjon?"

"Hello to you, Father."

"Ah . . . yes, hello. What's this about children?"

"Sage and I have decided to adopt a boy and a girl."

"What? Well, that might be just the thing. Whenever your mother became fidgety we had children. Calmed her right down. What? What do you mean, it drove you crazy? Heppie, don't talk nonsense. Stop interrupting . . ."

Ross choked back a laugh. It was always like this when he spoke to his parents. Both of them would talk at once.

"There. Is that better? I hooked the phone into the desk speaker. Your mother wants to talk at the same time as I do," the elder Tempest grumbled into the phone, his voice booming as if he were in an echo chamber.

"Hello, dear. Do tell us about the children. When will you be bringing them to Long Island? Will you commute? Surely it will be too difficult."

"Mother, the children are fine and I will tell you more about them when I'm home. For the time being we'll be living here. I will be coming into Manhattan at least once a week, so I will see you then."

"What about your home here?"

"We haven't worked that out yet."

"When are we to see the children?" His mother's voice rose several decibels.

"Uh . . . at Thanksgiving, I should think."

"Thanksgiving! That's months away. Ross, I don't like it." His mother only called him Ross when she was angry with him. It had been her father-in-law's first name and she had disliked him for his cigar smoking and womanizing, among other things. When she had married her husband she had thought to reform the widower, but she had been unable to handle her high-rolling relative-by-marriage. Now in his nineties, he lived in a palatial home in Palm Beach, Florida, keeping both a mistress and a houseful of pedigreed hunting dogs.

"Mother, Sage and I have a few things to work out. We need time to do it. We want to be with the children and see if we can mend our fences at the same time."

"Oh."

"Good for you, Sinjon. I like Sage. You keep in touch and give our best to her."

"Thanks, Father. I will."

Ross turned away from the phone, rocking back on the swivel chair behind the desk in the study, thinking about his parents and his family in general. Had they smothered Sage by their overwhelming desire to have the world revolve at their speed? Ross shook his head. No matter what his parents or his sisters and brothers-in-law had done, Sage wouldn't have been affected by it if she had felt confident in his love. Ross slapped his hand on the desktop. The top drawer of the desk slid open from the force of his blow. "Good Lord!" Thoughts of Sage and their past life fled as he looked at the bunched bundles of invoices jammed into the drawer. "She's been putting off doing the bills." Ross chuckled, remembering how he would find her checkbook in disarray, how she would write notes to herself in the columns, and how the whole thing was an indecipherable morass. He lifted the drawer out of its place, carrying it out of the room and down the corridor to the master bedroom. He knew the children would have rested and had their dinner and no doubt would be waiting for the babysitter to come. He took a detour through the kitchen and great room to check on them. Only the dog saw him. The children were glued to a cartoon of Charlie Brown on television. The dog's tail thumped once.

Ross smiled at the children and then walked quickly down the corridor leading to the bedroom. He stopped on the threshold, feeling his mouth and face relax in a smile. "You look wonderful in those undies, darling."

Sage spun around to face him, her eyes fixing on the drawer he was carrying. "Those are my bills."

Ross nodded. "Your unpaid ones, I assume?"

"Some are paid," she told him, on the defensive.

"Would you like to hire a good bookkeeper? A dollar a week and I'm yours."

"You wouldn't want to do the books for the Gasthaus . . . would you?" Hope warred with the feeling that she should remain aloof from Ross businesswise.

"Darling, you know I'm qualified to do your books." He saw the myriad feelings flash across her face. "You can always fire me if I don't do a good job."

"You went to Oxford. You have two master's degrees, one of them in business," she mused, then sighed. "I suppose it would be foolish to turn down this chance. Gusti has been saying we should hire an accounting firm. But they're so expensive."

"And my price is right."

"True." Sage nodded. "I'll do it!" She beamed at Ross, then frowned. "Could there be a conflict of interest here? You being my—my—"

"What? Husband? Live-in friend? Lover?"

"Forget I asked," Sage finished limply, all at once aware that Ross had moved closer, his eyes roving her body, his hands reaching out to her. "Have you heard one word I've said?"

"Of course. Do you take me for some sort of Dr. Lech? Who would only care about your body and getting it into bed?"

Sage fought it, but laughter bubbled out of her. "How did you remember Dr. Lecher, from my English course? Poor Dr. Adams, he just couldn't stop drooling over the nubile students."

"I sympathized with him fully." He leaned down and took her lower lip into his mouth. "You feel so silky." He kissed her, enjoying the feel of her lips and the tender recesses of her mouth. Without freeing himself from her he spoke. "Of course I know my duties as bookkeeper. You'll be impressed with my efficiency, but I might make passes at the boss."

Sage had trouble forming her words when his tongue kept tracing her lips. "How will you have the time? And still maintain your position with Worldwide Temp?"

"Easy." His breath entered her mouth, tickling her down to her toes. "I'll just do your books on those long, lonely evenings when you're at the restaurant. Some nights I'll be accompanying you there, just to check on the business, of course."

"Of course." Sage sagged against him, her arms lifting to clasp at his waist.

"What-at ar-re you do-ing?" Tad's monosyllabic shout drove them apart like a wedge. Tad glared at Ross.

"I'm kissing Mommy," Ross told him. "Daddies always do that with Mommies."

"A-re you ou-ur daddy?"

"Yes," Ross said firmly, ignoring the frantic signaling from Sage.

She turned away so that Tad couldn't read her lips. "You shouldn't have said that. You'll get his hopes up—"

"Don't be ridiculous," Ross snapped back. "I won't have these children thinking I'm some kind of night visitor who slips away at first light. It's not healthy for them—or me."

"I didn't mean . . ." Sage's voice trailed off helplessly at his stare.

"Drop it, Sage." Ross pulled her close, kissed her hard. Then he swiveled toward the boy, lifting him high in the air. "And Daddies also toss boys into the air." Ross didn't do that but he hugged Tad before placing him on the floor again. "I'll start working through this drawer." Picking up the desk drawer, he swung out of the room.

"Mommy? Is Lau-rie com-ing to-night?"

"Yes." Sage had a hard time concentrating as Tad followed her to her dressing table, chattering at her all the time she donned the light makeup she used in the evening when she went to the restaurant.

When she and the boy left the bedroom and went down the hallway leading to the living room, she could hear Laurie laughing. The sudden constriction in her chest surprised her. That she had always been possessive of Ross was not news to her, but that she would be jealous when he was talking to another female did stun her. "I am not infantile," she told herself, "nor will I act like it."

"Wh-ah-t did you say?" Tad's loud voice was evident to those in the room.

"Nothing. Just talking to myself," Sage dissembled, irked with herself.

They walked into the room to see the three people there facing them and watching.

"Hi," Tad said to Laurie, grinning at the college-age girl, who grinned back.

Ross saw the set of Sage's shoulders and knew she was irritated. He reviewed the facts at hand and came up with an answer that pleased him. He walked over to her, bent to kiss her, then let his mouth slide to her ear. "It drives me crazy when you get jealous."

Sage wanted to paste him one right on the nose. Instead, she placed her medium-high heel right on his instep and put all her weight behind it. "How sexy," she said on a long breath, batting her lashes at him as she saw his eyes flicker at the pressure.

"It will be tonight when I get you into bed, sweetheart. I intend to nibble on your glorious buns for hours." He took her gasp into his mouth, chuckling when he heard Tad's loud response.

"Dad-dies do that," Tad solemnly informed Laurie. "I don't kno-ow why."

Sage pulled back from Ross, her breathing ragged, aware that her hair was loose from its chignon and that Pip was taking in everything goggle-eyed and alert. "Well, ah, it's time for me to go." She coughed to clear the squeak from her voice.

Laurie watched them, her eyes bright.

"I'll drive you."

Sage swung to face Ross, openmouthed. "I always drive myself," she managed.

Ross nodded. "I know that." His voice was bland. "After Laurie leaves for school, we'll have to work out something different, but as long as she's still here, I'll drive you." He went over to Pip and lifted the child, kissing her on both cheeks and the forehead. "Be good for Daddy. I'll come back and tuck you in."

"I can drive—" Sage began, then closed her mouth when she saw the determination in his face.

"My mom always worries about you driving alone so late," Laurie offered.

Sage smiled weakly, then kissed each of the children, left instructions about the television watching, then preceded Ross, her head high, out the door to the car.

"I think you can stand the luxury of the Cadillac tonight." Ross steered her away from the Cherokee to the other side of the roomy garage, where the Eldorado sat in gleaming splendor. "I'm going back to the city on Wednesday after the kids start school, but I'll be back on Thursday."

Sage felt a surge of dizzying relief. He would be back the next day! Then she had an overwhelming wish to be able to stand behind herself and aim a good kick to her backside. She was a grown woman with a thriving business, independent and doing well, but she had been a pushover for Ross and now she was mooning over him like a teenager.

Ross felt a rush of pleasure at being with her in the air-conditioned comfort of the luxury vehicle. "I'm going to drive my Ferrari back here and have your Maserati sent. I'll leave the other cars at the house."

"You still live in that big house of yours?"

"Ours. That house belongs to both of us. Yes, that's still my address." He steeled his voice, hearing the quiver of anger there. "I admit that I've spent more time in our apartment in Manhattan this past year." He shrugged. "And quite a bit of time in the cottage."

"The cottage?" Sage echoed, recalling in a flash of memory the times they'd spent there, making love, talking.

"Yes."

"You sound martyred." The wrenching recollections made her voice sharper than she wanted.

"Do I?" he drawled silkily. "And you make it sound as though I were a man who would take a punch and go down." His eyes glittered at her in jewellike menace.

Sage caught her breath. "I know otherwise. You are a man who has always evened the score."

"Right, darling."

"What have you in mind for me?" She faced her lover.

"Night after night of loving, sweetheart. What else?"

His words said one thing, his tone told her that he was going to stretch her on the rack and keep her there. "Nothing," Sage mumbled. Why had she chosen to ride the razor's edge? What masochistic flaw did she have running through her psyche that made her respond to this man? A man who took up every gauntlet thrown down in front of him. *Lord*, she whispered to herself, agonized, *I'll be a white-haired hag in no time.*

"Who's being the martyr now?"

"You are Svengali himself."

"Right."

Her head swiveled his way. "You admit it! Doesn't it make you feel guilty to know you've manipulated me?"

"Do you feel guilty for doing the same thing to me?"

"Never!"

"Never that you don't feel guilty or never that you don't regret feeling guilty for manipulating me?"

"Stop trying to mix me up," she fumed, hopping out of the car as soon as he parked in the lot behind the kitchen door at the Gasthaus. "And no one but Zeus could manipulate you." She walked away, head high.

"Are you feeding me sauerbraten this evening?" he called after her as he climbed from the Cadillac.

"Don't try to change the subject." She kept moving, not turning to look at him when he laughed.

Once in the kitchen, Sage forgot their wrangling and went at once to her cubbyhole to one side of the main kitchen area. She scanned the usual list of reservations and the dinner preferences that many of them included, then set her mind to the sauces, most German, some French, that she would be concocting that evening.

Gusti put his head in the doorway and smiled at Sage. "Why didn't you tell us that your so wonderful husband was going to be our business manager?"

Sage looked blankly at her tall yet plump friend. "I'm delighted you're pleased. He told me he was going to sort out the bills I had brought home to do. Where is he?"

"In the office, up to his armpits in paper and books." Gusti shuddered. "What a life, working with numbers and ledgers. That is the stuff that hell is made of."

"I couldn't agree more." Sage laughed. "That is the

one flaw in our relationship, my friend. Neither of us likes to balance the books."

"Then please don't talk your husband out of doing it. I'm willing to pay any fee he asks."

Sage felt the smile slip away when Gusti left the small sauce kitchen. What was Ross up to? Was he going to tell her that her restaurant venture was only marginally successful? She knew that! But there was growth here too! She argued with herself, then gave a huge sigh and pushed the argument to the back of her mind.

She blanked her mind to Ross and concentrated on the sauce for an order of *Königsberger Klopse*, spicy beef, pork, and veal croquettes, adding the capers at the very end. She completed the recipe, placing the croquettes, which had been prepared by one of the other cooks, on a hot platter, then drizzled the hot sauce over all. She garnished the platter with parsley and lemon and orange curls, then rang the bell. "Oh, that was quick," she said, turning, expecting to see Ludwig, Gusti's brother. Ross stood there instead, staring at the hot platter she was holding with her cooking mitts.

"That is beautiful . . . but too heavy. Let me—"

"No . . . no"—Sage swayed away from him, somehow balancing the platter—"you'll be burned. This is very hot."

Ludwig swung his head through the pass-through. "My order? Ah, as usual, a masterpiece. Let me take it. My customer is beginning to chew on the tablecloth." Ludwig took the platter, looking apologetic. "You might get a few more orders. Mr. Jensen has been raving about our *Klopse* to all who would listen." He gave her a rakish grin and swung away with his burden.

"Could I put in an order?" Ross leaned over and wiped a damp tendril of hair from her eyes. "You look cute in that hair net."

"Like a good German hausfrau." Sage smiled up at

him, then removed the disposable food gloves she used for working. She generally went through three or four pairs in an evening.

"Something like that." Ross stepped closer to her. "Thought you didn't have an ounce of German blood."

"I don't." Sage leaned her warm forehead against his chest. Even with the air conditioning it could get warm in her corner of the kitchen. "But I did pick up a few pointers in cooking when I was an exchange student."

Ross hugged her and looked around him. "This place is spotlessly clean and you have marvelous kitchen hygiene." Ross tightened his hands at her waist, resting his cheek on her hair net.

"Thanks to Oma Baumann. She and her grandchildren scrub the place from stem to stern every day, and I mean every day." Sage lifted her head and grinned at him. "If she sees a speck of dirt, heads roll." She could feel Ross's rumbling chuckle under her cheek.

Ludwig stuck his head around the corner. "What did I tell you? Three orders of *Klopse*, please."

Sage pushed back from Ross, washed her hands, donned fresh gloves, took the mix out of the refrigerator, and swiftly began the croquettes, even as Liesl, Gusti's niece and Helga's sister, came up behind her, slipped on gloves, and smoothly moved into her place so that Sage could get right at the sauce. She was aware every moment that Ross hadn't taken his eyes from her.

"Hi. I'm Liesl." The young girl threw Ross a grin, not breaking stride in her work as she placed the meat molds on a tray and slipped them into the hot oven.

"I'm Ross. Hello."

"I know. Oma says you are going to be the boss man of the books." Liesl laughed when Ross did.

"It's not that bad, but I hope to find a few places where we might cut corners and save money."

We! Did he say we? Sage ruminated. She felt a fluttery

sensation in her middle, then shook her head. Stop acting like a fool, she castigated herself, almost burning the delicate sauce she was making. In time, she lifted the pan, added the capers, then poured it over the hot meat croquettes.

Liesl quickly put it in the oven again for a few seconds, brought it out, and left to get back to the main kitchen. Ludwig appeared at the window again.

"The same again. Six times." He grinned at Sage and took the hot platter Liesl had removed from the oven.

Ross frowned when he saw her swirl to the fridge to get the meat mixture. "I'll help."

"You will? But—but you don't—"

"I'll help."

Much to Sage's surprise he did help. While she was at it she made an extra batch of the recipe for Ross and while she was putting the food on the plates for Ludwig she added a large single order to another hot platter.

Ludwig took his.

Sage turned with the other hot platter. "This is for you."

Ross smiled in lazy admiration. "I will eat it if you sit with me and have some too."

Sage opened her mouth to tell him that she had to stay on the job when Oma appeared, frowning at her.

"Time for you to rest, Saggy." Oma reached for one of the throwaway aprons that were used for the cooks, then washed her hands, powdering them and slipping on the gloves. "I will make the sauces. Go with your man." She pronounced it "mahn."

"Thank you, Oma."

"A woman should be with her man."

"Thank you, Oma," Ross repeated, chuckling. "I agree." His spate of German had the older lady chortling and pointing at Sage.

"Stop that." Sage spoke from the side of her mouth as she passed him.

Ross took the hot platter. Sage carried a basket of dark bread and a bowl of *Spätzle*, the lovely German pasta that Oma made fresh daily for the patrons of the Gasthaus, to the small table out in the main dining room that was often used by members of the family. It was near the kitchen and screened from the rest of the room by a huge fern.

The buzz of conversation and laughter filled the large room and the small anterooms leading from it.

Ross helped her to her chair, then seated himself, looking from the food to her. "This is wonderful. Why didn't we cook *à deux* on Long Island?"

Sage leaned her chin on her hand, studying him. "Many reasons. Generally when I cooked we had a few friends to dinner . . . and our paths didn't cross that often when I could have done it for us." She shrugged. "So it was simpler to let Haddon handle it when we dined alone."

A shadow flickered deep in his eyes. Then he smiled at her. "Let me help you to some of this."

Sage sighed and nodded. "I hope I can do it justice. So many times I can't eat after being around the many food smells. It seems to block the appetite, rather than enhance it, for me."

"Is that why you're a few too many pounds under your normal weight?"

"One of them." And there was also the reason that she hadn't been able to eat after she had left their home. She didn't tell him that or that she had gained some of the weight back.

"Ummm. This is wonderful." Ross grinned at her, his fork poised in his hand. "Eat up, lady. I know the chef and she's great."

Sage felt a flood of pride at his words.

When Ludwig came by the table with a bottle wrapped in a napkin, he grinned at them. "Oma says you must have the crisp Riesling with the *Klopse*." With a quick turn, he uncapped the bottle and drew the cork. Flourishing the wineglasses, he poured and set one in front of Ross and one in front of Sage. *"Der Appetit kommt beim Essen,"* he whispered to her.

Ross's eyes narrowed on her. "Why did he say that appetite comes from eating? Have you been on some ridiculous diet?"

"Not really." Sage sighed. "I haven't wanted to eat that much, but my appetite has grown lately."

Ross stared at her for long moments, as though he read into her soul. "I see."

"Children can keep you busy," Sage continued lamely.

"True."

Sage lowered her head and tackled the succulent, tender food on her plate, surprising herself by the surge of hunger that assailed her.

Ross watched her. She was very vulnerable and so easily hurt, he thought. Making her happy had always been high on his list of priorities. How had he let such a precious thing slip from his grasp? He could feel his insides knot at the thought of being apart from her, estranged . . . maybe even divorced. He wasn't about to let that happen.

"What are you thinking?"

Ross looked around the room, digging in his mind for an alternative thought. "It would be great if you had a dance band here."

Sage nodded. "We've considered it. There's a young man who lives about a mile from us, who attends the music school at the local university. He and some of his friends are anxious to make money playing gigs."

Ross winced.

"Not hard rock." Sage laughed. "Swing music from

the thirties has become the vogue with many of the young people. I've heard them play and they're good."

Ross shrugged. "Why not give them a chance on the weekends?"

"We could," Sage said hesitantly.

"It would be great." Ross poured a bit more of the Riesling into her glass, then grinned at her. "And yes, I do remember that you're not much of a drinker, but I think the wine is good for you with your meal." He scowled for a moment. "You work too hard."

"I agree." Sage laughed at him. "But I like what I do," she hurried to explain when she saw his scowl deepen.

Ludwig came to the table. "Food good?" He looked at Ross.

"Very good." Ross wiped his mouth, trying to mask his annoyance at the interruption. That was the trouble! He was never alone with her. He itched with guilty memory when he recalled the many times he had worked late, then joined a few of the staff for drinks before going home. No other woman had ever come into his sphere, though he had been tempted a time or two when Sage had begun to draw away from him. It bothered him more than he cared to accept that it was only now, after he had been served with divorce papers, that he was actively pursuing and wooing the woman he had married . . . the woman he loved.

"Ross?"

"What?" He dabbed at his lips with his napkin again to cover his confusion. "You said something to me?"

Sage laughed aloud. "And you used to tell me I was the dreamer."

"So you were . . . still are." And he knew he didn't want her any other way.

Sage gestured to Ludwig, who was still hovering at the table, and whispered to him, "Ludwig says that he can call Wally Predmore and ask him if his group can play this Friday evening. What do you think?"

Ross felt his heart skip out of rhythm. Her eyes were like stars! She had included him in the decision. All his years of making corporate decisions that affected thousands and thousands of lives he had handled with ease. Having Sage include him in such a minor happening had flooded him with delight.

"Why don't you mention it to Gusti and see what he thinks?" Ross took hold of her arm when she would have risen. "First we'll finish our dinner. Then do it."

"I'll tell Gusti what you said, Sage," Ludwig said breezily, then sailed away, his towel flapping from his arm.

Sage cocked her head and stared at Ross. "Why do I get the feeling that you're angry?"

"Not angry. Irritated. I want more time alone with you, beautiful lady." It delighted him when she reddened and smiled. He took her hand and lifted it, pressing his mouth into the palm.

Neither noticed when someone approached the table.

"I think it's a great idea—oops. I have come at a bad time." An irrepressible Gusti smiled down into Ross's now-glowering face.

"Yes."

"No you haven't." Sage shook her head at her husband, feeling airy and girlish. "Should we call him, do you think?"

"Ludwig's doing it now."

"Great." Sage clapped her hands.

"I'll get back to the kitchen." Gusti grinned at Ross.

"Something is burning, no doubt," he urged dryly.

"Ross!"

"Do I make an appointment to be alone with you?" he asked her as Gusti ambled away, laughing.

"He is a very dear friend, as is his family."

"Then he becomes my friend, too, but I still want to be alone with you."

"I'd like that."

Ross paused in the act of drinking his wine.

"Well, I'm human too," she added.

"Are you, my darling?" He tried to clear his throat of its huskiness.

She nodded.

He reached for her hand again.

This time she put both of hers into his.

"I want a life with you, Sage."

She blinked rapidly, trying to clear the unaccustomed sting from her eyes. "It will be hard work."

"Very."

"We're volatile."

"Especially with each other."

She nodded. "Have you—were there many—" She pressed her lips together, shaking her head. "Not my business."

"I had dinner with a few women. . . ." He felt the rush of blood up his face.

"I went to dinner a couple of times."

He cleared his throat, his grip tightening on her. "Sage, I won't make any excuses."

"I know."

"I feel we have to be open with one another." He swallowed. "As I mentioned before I tried dating other women and with some I was very tempted. They were beautiful and desirable. I tried to erase my feelings for you. It didn't work. When I kissed them I saw you and it was no good." He lifted her now-cold hands to his mouth, his eyes fixed on hers. "We can hurt each other."

"I agree."

"Even now when we're being open with each other, it won't always be smooth."

Seven

The summer days drifted into autumn. Green leaves turned russet, gold, and red, their dry rattles like a background for a ghost movie.

Some days it seemed to Ross that he had never lived anywhere but the house in Irondequoit. He often resented the Tuesdays and Wednesdays and sometimes Thursday mornings he spent in Manhattan. Not only hadn't his work suffered with his absence, it had given his brother-in-law Barry, who was a vice president, special incentive to do well. Also, Ross had developed a rising interest in the restaurant business. He smiled to himself as he drove through the wooded lanes that led to the house. Of course one of the reasons his interest in the restaurant had sharpened had been Sage. He had all but forgotten his many reasons for "getting even" with her for leaving him. Now he concentrated his every move on getting her back and keeping her.

Children! Ross shook his head as he slowed the car because of a deer grazing in a neighbor's front yard. Sage had cautioned him about their unpredictable jumps that took them into the side of a car. Children! Tad and Pip. Those ridiculous nicknames that now seemed not only fitting but attractive. They had so climbed through his every pore in a little over two months that he sometimes had to remind himself that they were neither his nor Sage's natural children.

He thought of his parents and frowned. His mother was growing increasingly edgy with him and with Sage because no move had been made to take the children to Long Island for a visit.

"You still insist on Thanksgiving, Sinjon?" His mother had called him at the office on Wednesday afternoon, her voice reedy and tight over the phone.

"It's only three weeks away, Mother."

"And I think it's thoughtless of you to deny me my grandchildren." She took a deep breath. "That's what I told Sage when I called her today."

"You what?" Ross sounded out each vowel and consonant.

"Don't you use that threatening tone to me, Ross St. John."

"Mother, what did Sage say?"

"Not much, just that you were bringing the children at Thanksgiving. I am very disappointed in that girl—"

"Sage is a woman, not a girl."

"Don't bandy words with me, Sinjon. I told her that I thought it was inconsiderate of her to deny me my grandchildren. What did she mean when she said that she wasn't sure they were my grandchildren? She is married to you still. Any children of issue or adoption belong to you both. I called Wilbert Fitch and checked."

"Mother! Listen to me. Any problems that Sage and I

have will be ironed out by us and by no one else. I'll allow interference from no one—"

The phone had banged down in his ear before he could say any more.

Now as he pulled in the driveway and saw Morris the turkey strutting toward the car, ready to give the Ferrari the same treatment he gave any low-slung vehicle, Ross felt an amused sense of homecoming.

He jammed on the brakes and jumped from the car to try and forestall the determined gobbler. "Hold it right here, Morris. It's one thing to do a tattoo on a Cherokee . . . and another to do it on a Ferrari. So, let's forget it." Ross danced in front of the bobbing and weaving bird.

"I told you that he would go after it." Sage laughed as she walked out into the yard, shrugging on an Irish sweater that Ross had given her years ago.

"Being an 'I told you so' is crass," Ross said huffily, trying to outmaneuver the fast and agile wild fowl. It delighted him that she was there, laughing so unrestrainedly. She had come to meet the car, to meet him, he told himself, refusing to accept any of the other myriad reasons that Sage could have for coming out of the house. "Kids still at school?"

"Yes. This evening is Parents' Night. Will you come?" Sage knew the answer before he nodded. Ross had filled his life with the children. They were with him every moment that he was home. Sage was awed by the progress that Pip had made with him. More than once she had lifted her arms to him so that he could carry her, and Ross had talked of nothing else for days.

"I'll be damned if I'll let him get the Ferrari." Ross leaned back against the hood as Sage approached the big bird with a handful of seed.

Distracted, Morris ignored his out-of-breath adversary in lieu of better game. Sunflower seeds!

Sage looked up at Ross after putting the seeds on the

ground for the bird and laughed. "Better put the car away."

"Right." Ross glowered at the turkey, then pushed away from the car. "First I have to kiss my live-in lady. I haven't seen her in two and a half days. Miss me?"

"Could be."

"Tell me," he growled into her neck.

"Actually, the children missed you." Sage felt herself lifted against his body. "I hardly noticed you'd gone."

"Brat. Admit the bed was cold."

"I'll buy an electric blanket."

Ross shook his head. "You don't like them."

"True." She cupped his face with her hands. "Rough two days?"

Ross shrugged. "We've been taking the heat from a few of the investors because we decided to close the plant in Johannesburg." He put his arm around her and turned her toward the Ferrari. He steered her around to the passenger side and put her in the car. He grinned at her nonplussed look. "You're the one who told me to put the car away."

Sage watched him walk around the front of the car, his rakish smile coming through the windshield and heating her. How could one man have so much sexual power?

He slipped in beside her and took hold of her knee.

"You'd better hurry," Sage said, chuckling and pointing to the big bird, who had finished his seed and was looking around for more game.

"Monster." Ross accelerated around the bird, seeing him gather himself for a jump at the car. "Dammit, no one would believe me if I told them that I have to run a turkey gauntlet before I can put my car in the garage," Ross muttered, activating the garage door so that it closed in front of the running turkey.

"Not to worry. The doors won't come down on Morris. I

had special ones installed that stop moving the moment they touch anything." Sage tittered behind her hand.

"Too bad," Ross growled, turning to look at her, unable to mask the smile that stretched across his face. He hadn't known that the happiness they had experienced these past months was possible. They had never laughed so much . . . or loved so much. He could feel his hands and feet tingle with the need to hold her and make love to her right at that very moment. He shot out his wrist and glanced at his watch. "By my calculations we have an hour and a half before the children get off the school bus."

"Bright man."

Ross threw back his head and laughed. "Sarcastic little devil." He hopped out of his side and rushed around to open her door, pulling her out and up into his arms when she wasn't fast enough. "Payback time." He thrust his tongue into her mouth, feeling the answering push of hers against it. "Lord, I needed you, wanted you."

"Me too. Oma said that I wasn't to think of you anymore when I made the Alsatian sauce. Twice last week it came out lumpy." Laughter bubbled out of her, her body bumping against his.

"Hey, woman, pay attention. You have two children and a live-in lover to support. We don't come cheap," Ross said to her, leading her into the house and down the hall to the bedroom wing.

"Ya get what ya pay for," Sage parodied, ducking away from Ross when he rounded on her.

"And what would you know about getting what you paid for in the love department, sweetheart?" The silky smoothness of Ross's voice menaced the air around them.

Sage was at once titillated and irritated. "Have I ever asked you for details about the women you took to dinner while we were apart?"

Ross stared at her for a moment, took a deep breath, and shook his head, one hand threading through his hair in rough fashion. "We discussed this and it should be dropped. The question was unfair, but that doesn't stop the morbid curiosity I have about you during the time we were apart." He smiled ruefully. "This digging and peeling away at each other has been beneficial, but it has been a Pandora's box too." He began to undress with his usual lightning precision when Sage was near him and they were alone. He hated anything between them but skin. He stood before her nude, wishing she would hurry and disrobe. "I've learned more about you and about us in the last months than I knew existed, but I've also found a more jealous, possessive streak in me that I didn't know I had."

"Tell me about it," Sage muttered, biting her lip as she thought of the many nights she tossed and turned when they were apart, wondering who Ross might be with. She stared at him. "Even before I came here, I'd wonder if you were seeing women at work who attracted you, if there was anyone at the club—" She swallowed, shaking her head. "I had to leave because I was starting to question my sanity." Her laughter had a tremor in it when she saw Ross's eyes soften and he started around the bed toward her.

"I'll help you undress." He leaned over her, kissing her shoulder as the last of her clothing dropped in a pool at her feet.

"Let me love you, lady mine."

"Please do." Sage felt the sensual thunder in her being as she always did when Ross was close to her. "We've certainly made love more than we ever have since our honeymoon."

Ross nodded. "We put our feelings for each other on the wrong rung of the ladder."

"A-about the middle, I think." Sage gasped when he

reached out a gentle forefinger and thumb and closed them around one nipple.

"Right behind social scene and what trip to take," Ross went on, his eyes never leaving her body. "You used to have a slightly rounded tummy." His other hand made slow whorls on her abdomen. "Now it's concave."

"Children keep you on your toes." Sage's eyelids felt like lead.

"Husbands keep you off them," Ross intoned in imitation.

Sage gave a shaky chuckle.

Ross felt his heart thud like a hammer against an anvil. He knelt in front of her still-standing body, pressing his face to her middle, feeling her shudder with the beginning of the sexual excitement that filled them both every time they touched one another.

"Ross," Sage said softly.

"I'm here with you. All the way."

"I know."

He caught her sagging body and lifted her, so that they both fell on the bed together, face-to-face.

In quiet wonder they scaled and rappeled each other's bodies, not quite sure why the delight was greater each time but happy that the feeling in one was engendered in the other.

Ross touched her skin with his tongue, taking her hips into his hands and cuddling her closer to him. "I can't believe how fragile you are, yet you're as strong as Athena, the goddess of war."

Sage studied the sensual slash of his mouth and felt the quivering response in every extremity. "You're pretty strong yourself."

Every night and day that they'd been together since the trip to the State Fair, they had made love. Not since their honeymoon had they concentrated such energy on each other. It had stunned Sage that each time was better, that she wanted more and more of Ross.

"Sage . . ." Ross groaned against her breast when her hands feathered over him.

She parroted the love answer he had given her. "Yes, I'm here."

They clutched each other with newfound fervor, hands touching everywhere, body locked to body.

They descended in shuddering gentle violence, holding and soothing each other.

Ross lifted his head from her breast, his eyes glinting over her. "A man could die with you loving him."

"And a woman could die from love of you." Sage sighed.

They rose as one, washing and dressing side by side, looking at one another often and smiling.

Sage stood at the stove, stirring simmering homemade Bavarian potato soup. It was the same recipe she used at the restaurant, and it was a very nourishing and tasty meal. She ladled out two large bowls and carried them over to Tad and Ross. "Here you are. I'm going to meet Pip's bus. I'll be right back."

"I'll go with you," Ross said, putting his cracker down and rising.

"No, no, you stay with Tad and continue this feast. I'll be right back."

Sage laughed when Morris the turkey joined her and the dog as she walked down the driveway. "Someone is going to have me certified one day if they catch me walking with a wild turkey and a golden retriever and conversing with them to boot." She flung her arms up in the air, staring at the cerulean sky through the golden, red, and russet leaves falling slowly to the ground. "I am so happy," she told the stillness of the day, the quiet of the curving drive taking her voice and bouncing it back to her.

Just as she reached the end of the drive, the yellow school bus halted, its red lights flashing the signal for traffic to stop both ways. The door opened and the driver stepped down with Pip, smiling and waving to Sage.

Sage opened her arms to the little girl, not expecting her to run into them, but gratified when Pip lifted her arms to be hugged. "Darling, darling. Someday you'll talk to me . . . and not just scattered words here and there," she murmured to the little girl, holding her small frame for a moment longer. She released the child, then took her mittened hand. "It's getting so cold." They hurried along the drive to the house. "Come inside and I'll give you some soup. Daddy and Tad are having some." Sage felt her body jerk as she looked down at the child. Had it been her imagination or had Pip smiled?

Once inside they removed their coats. Before they could hang them up, Ross was there, lifting the little girl and kissing her as he always did.

"How's Daddy's best girl today? Were you the smartest in the school? I'll bet you were." He kissed her again.

When Pip locked her hands around his neck and pressed her face against him, both Sage and Ross were still as statues.

"That was no accident," Sage said shakily.

"I agree." Ross reached out a hand without releasing his hold on the child, and pulled Sage close to him. Then he swiveled his glance toward the child, who was still manacled to him. "Daddy has some nice soup for his big girl." Ross freed Sage's hand, and preceded her down the hall to the kitchen, still murmuring to Pip.

"Happiness is being with Ross," Sage mutterd to herself, entering the kitchen and looking at the three of them hunched over the breakfast bar. Ross was giving his cooler soup to Pip, then ladling more into another bowl.

He looked up and grinned at her. "Sit down and join us." He pulled another stool close to his and patted the seat.

The four of them ended up having a very eclectic meal of soup, graham crackers, carrot sticks, pickles, and assorted foods they scavenged from the fridge.

Ross sat back and patted his middle, grinning at Tad and Pip. "That was great."

"Ye-es." Tad grinned at him, patting his sister on the back.

Pip offered Ross the last carrot stick on her plate.

In the act of pouring tea, Sage inhaled a deep breath and watched, so enthralled with the child's gesture that she had to take quick measures to keep from overfilling Ross's cup.

"Go-od," Tad told his sister.

"Very good, indeed, Daddy's big girl." Ross leaned down and took the carrot between his teeth, his nose almost touching Pip's, his gaze holding hers. "I've never had a nicer gift."

Pip didn't smile but she leaned toward Ross, putting her weight on him.

Sage struggled to hold back tears as she turned toward the stove again. Putting down the teapot, she pressed her fist to her mouth and stared at the tall crystal pepper mill that sat in its own niche above the stove.

"Are you crying, darling?" Ross whispered at her back.

Sage nodded.

"They've gone to play that new spelling game you bought them, so you can turn around and be teary just for me." Ross chuckled into her hair when she turned into his chest and sobbed. "I feel a little weepy myself."

"It's wonderful, isn't it?"

"Outstanding." He kissed her nose. "And we'll keep taking baby steps forward with her until she is yelling and playing just like any other child . . . maybe even as well-adjusted as her brother."

Sage felt a smile stretch her face even as the tears dribbled down her cheeks. "He is special, isn't he?"

"Very. He embodies all the courage that any man would want his son to have. He has a heads-up view of life that accepts his deafness but defies anyone to tell him that it slows him up."

"Because it doesn't." Sage gave a shaky laugh.

Ross touched her nose with an index finger. "He's intrepid, like his mama."

She grinned up at him. "You've called me many things . . . but never that."

"I'm getting to know you."

"Yes." She felt the smile slip from her face.

"And you're getting to know me."

Sage was still for a moment. "I do admit there are sides to you I hadn't known."

"No more hiding." He pressed his forehead down to hers.

"There's no place to hide anymore."

"Not for us."

"Damn the torpedoes."

"You mustn't talk about my family like that."

Chuckles reverberated from her body to his.

"Please do that again." Ross rolled his eyes.

She pinched his side gently. "Lecher."

"You mean you didn't know?"

"I had an idea."

"Silly lady. I've been lusting after you since you ran into me when you were a law intern." He held her tighter. "Then we went on that foolish skating party that your school was having and you fell face first on the ice. From that moment I was gone."

"That long?" Pleasure rippled through her at the thought.

"Yes."

"Why did it take you so long to propose?"

"All of two days after I met you?"

She cocked her head to one side. "It seemed like years at the time. I was sure one of my very sexy housemates would floor you."

"Well-l-l, I looked at them all—ouch, you're pinching too hard." He nipped gently at her lips with his teeth, but made no move to push her hands from his body.

"Poor baby."

The phone rang at her elbow, making her jump and arch her back away from the sound.

"Ummm. Lovely, darling." Ross tightened his hold on her.

Sage laughed at him and picked up the phone. "Yes. Thanks, Nell. Yes, I'm sure the children will love it. Twenty minutes? We'll be ready." Sage replaced the receiver, turning to speak to Ross.

He took her words with his mouth, deepening the kiss when he felt her sag against him.

"Mom-my." Tad pulled on Sage's arm, grinning up at his parents. "Pi-ip says the phone rang."

Sage pulled back from Ross, not able to control the hectic color she knew was rising in her face. She patted at her hair and tried to straighten her clothes. She looked down at her son and nodded. "That was Mrs. Findlay. She is coming to get you and Pip so you can play with Jason and Melissa—"

"Wheeee!" Tad interrupted, then spun around and went to tell his sister.

Sage was conscious that Ross didn't take his eyes from her as they raced around getting the children dressed for their outing.

"Mom-my," Tad wailed when he saw the car in the

driveway, and Sage was still securing Pip's thermal gloves to the fastener on the sleeve of the snowsuit that she was wearing.

Sage stood back and looked at her little solemn-eyed child.

"She looks like a Christmas card," Ross said quietly at her back. Then he leaned over and lifted Pip and hugged her. He carried her out the front door to where Tad was dancing in excitement next to the Bronco. He was talking a blue streak to Jason and Melissa. Nell Findlay waved to Sage.

"No, Morris, you can't go," Ross told the strutting turkey. Morris pecked at the car and gobbled at the children.

Nell rolled her eyes toward Sage, then spoke to the wild fowl. "George says if you don't stop pecking at the Bronco, you're getting a muzzle."

"Good idea." Ross went forward, his hand outstretched. "Hello, I'm Ross Tempest, Sage's friend." He shot a glance at Sage and could hardly control his laughter when she glowered at him.

"Hi." Nell's eyes snapped with interest. "I'm her neighbor and friend too."

"We have something in common," Ross drawled, wrapping his arm around Sage when he saw her shiver in the cold. "Have a good time. Wave, darling." He chuckled.

"How can I went you have me swaddled in your coat?" She tried to continue glaring at him, but she couldn't hold back a smile.

"Shall we go back inside while I tell you what I thought the first and second times I saw you?"

Sage stared at him, then nodded slowly. "I've been finding out more things lately than I ever knew."

"And I decided when I was flying to New York last week

that you probably never knew the effect you had on me . . . because we were so formal with each other—"

"And passionate." Sage shivered over the word as she hurried into the house to the great room to sit in front of the fire.

"We were that." Ross chuckled, lifting her from the chair, then pulling her down with him to sit on the round Oriental rug in front of the raised brick hearth. He kissed her on the nose, then stared into the tongues of flame as though they had a picture he needed to see. "I had toyed with the idea of canceling a speech I was making at your college. That was why I was at Max's office. He had given a talk at the school a few months before, and I wanted to make sure that I wasn't going to overlap on what he had said. Then I saw you and I found out from Max that you attended Sarah Lawrence and that you would be returning to the campus. I had planned to speak on the future of women in business. After having had dinner with you, I knew the next day that I couldn't wait to get to Sarah Lawrence, make the speech, then go looking for you."

"I attended the lecture."

Ross shot her a heated glance. "I know. You were the one who staggered in late with the mountain of books and sat at the back of the class."

"Tell me about when you saw me later."

"I was watching the skating. Then you came down the ice and your laughter went right through me. I still like to hear you talk or sing." He grinned at her. "You started to do figure eights like your friend and ended up in a snowbank."

"You saw that and didn't pick me up." Sage yawned into his shirt.

"And I never told you the reason that I didn't was because I was hammered to the ground . . . by a laugh. I didn't take my eyes off you, even when the Neanderthal Man picked you up and carted you back onto the ice."

"If you're talking about Mel Sedgwick, I'll have you know all the girls were jealous that he was my boyfriend."

"He didn't have a forehead or a separation in his eyebrows," Ross said testily.

Sage laughed aloud. "He *was* a bit fierce-looking."

"All I did was stare at you, the same way I'd done when you were in class and when you fell in front of me in Max's outer office. In class you looked bored, then uncomfortable . . . because I didn't take my eyes from you."

Sage looked up at him, biting his chin. "I was worried that you could read my mind. I thought you were gorgeous."

"Did you?" Ross felt his heart pump out of rhythm at her words.

"Yes."

"When I stopped you when you were leaving class, you didn't look too pleased."

"I was scared to death you were going to tell me that you had decided I bored you after the dinner we'd shared."

Ross put his head on hers. "Oh, angel, I was going out of my mind because you were so young and I wanted to eat you up."

"Dinner had been fun."

"Eating deep-fried vegetables in a bucket was not my idea of a romantic dinner for two."

Sage closed her eyes and rubbed her middle. "I did so love deep-fried veggies."

"You have a stomach of iron."

"I remember sitting in your car and kissing you for one hour without breaking lip contact. Then you said—"

"I know," Ross interrupted. "What will we call our

firstborn son, I asked you." His mouth moved over her forehead.

"I thought of that so many times."

Ross turned her to face him. "You wanted children and I wanted children. We should have had more solid discussions about it. Why did we tap-dance around each other?"

Sage took a deep breath. "At first I was too afraid to break the pink bubble we lived in. Then, when I began to smother in it, I couldn't talk to you. I solved my dilemma by leaving."

"Shall we try to have a baby?"

Sage shot out of his arms, freezing in place, as though Ross had suggested they take a Kodiak bear for a stroll. "Children should be brought into—"

"Don't give me that stability crap, Sage." A muscle jumped at the side of his mouth when he spat the words at her. "We have a very solid home here. It's going to get better, not weaken."

"I want to believe that."

"Believe it. We're living together, but if we decide to marry—"

Sage interrupted this time. "We are married."

"If we decide to marry, it will be in a church with our children beside us. Either way we'll be together."

"Tough guy, huh?"

Ross gazed at her, hard amusement in his eyes. "Lady, if you want to see how tough I can be, just try getting away from me again."

A frisson of wariness ran from her neck to coccyx. "What would you do?"

"Try me," Ross snapped. Then he reached for her before she could react and pulled her across his lap. His hands feathered over her, telegraphing his rising passion. "I'll never let you leave me again. Never."

"What will you do? Beat me?" Sage asked, torn between laughter and irritation.

"No. I'll get down on my knees and beg you not to," Ross said quietly, his hand touching her breasts.

Sage gaped at him. "You wouldn't."

Ross shrugged. "As I said, try me."

Sage dug her nails into his neck, probing, touching, trying to mark him as hers. "I might get down there with you."

"Sounds exciting." His lazy power poured over her like lava.

Sage swallowed. "Doesn't it!"

He opened her blouse and pressed his mouth between her breasts. "I need nourishment." He pushed aside the lacy bra she was wearing and began to pull gently on one nipple.

"Ross," Sage sobbed.

"Yes, I'm here."

"I want it to be the way you say, but I'm fearful. What about Tad and Pip?"

Ross lifted his head, a mixture of passion and irritation replacing the loving glaze to his eyes. "Darling, they will always have primary place as our first children . . . but not when I'm making love to you. That belongs to us."

Sage attempted to smooth his hair ruffled by her restless hands. "Very wise." She gave a watery chuckle, feeling lighter. Problems were being put in their proper pigeonholes and brought down to size. They would be able to take them out when needed, scan them, and never allow them to balloon in their lives. . . .

"One other thing!" Ross took her lower lip into his mouth, worrying it gently with his teeth. "You're not allowed to let your mind wander when I'm seducing you," he snarled softly against her skin.

"Fine with me," Sage gasped as his mouth abraded

her skin, pulling and grasping at every pore, bringing sizzling life to every spot he touched.

"Touch me, Sage. I need that," he groaned against her hip.

Not hesitating, Sage unleashed her own strung-tight-as-wire feelings, letting them crash through all the fences she had built to protect herself and avalanche over both of them. Her hands were wild on him, pulling, prodding, caressing in a fevered way that she had never allowed herself before.

Cascade after cascade of emotion lifted them, flung them out on a limitless ocean. They were like paper boats tossed far out on a pond, tossing, turning, unanchored, their only hold to earth each other.

I love him, love him, love him, Sage's whole being cried out as she felt him enter her, take her on the rampage of love that left them both gasping for air, drained, emptied, but fulfilled.

Afterward, Ross rolled onto his back, taking her with him, letting her spawl across his chest. "I won't let you go, angel. Anything else you can ask me." It stunned him that he was more committed to her now than he had been just before they made love. It energized and weakened him to realize that only Sage had the power not only to wound but to destroy him.

Eight

There would be lots of snow for Thanksgiving! Sage joined the children on the hill in back of the house where they always went sledding.

The dog was chasing them on the hill as they went down on their stomachs, curving along the slope that widened at the bottom of a lovely, stream-bisected valley filled with fir and pine trees.

Sage looked up at the sky clouded with the softly falling flakes of white. Her heart thudded in painful awareness that Ross was up there, flying the plane himself in a snowstorm. She felt her insides shred and splinter at the thought of him coming down, not able to see the ground. . . . She swiped at her face with a mittened hand, trying to brush away the thoughts as well as the tears.

"Hey, lady, you're supposed to sit on that toboggan,

not just hold the towing rope," Ross said at her back, his shearling-coated arms wrapping around her.

"Ross!" she sobbed, turning in his arms and pressing her face into the softness of his jacket.

"What is it?" His arms tightened in alarm.

"It's snowing. I was worried. You were alone up there." Her staccato words were muffled in his chest. She felt his chest deflate with relief.

He lifted her chin with a bare hand, seeming impervious to the cold around them. "Nothing was going to keep me from you. Nothing ever will."

"Promise," Sage said, and gulped, her hands going around him in convulsive need.

"Cross my heart," he said, reciting the childish vow.

"I'll race you down the hill." She pushed back from him, delight flowing through her because he was with them again. She tried to grab the sled and push it toward the hill.

Ross swung her up and away from the sled, his hands grasping her waist. Then he sat down on the old-fashioned wooden toboggan with its well-padded cushioning and placed Sage in front of him. "Heads up down there, Pip," Ross called to the child at the bottom of the hill. He waited until she had gestured to her brother that they were coming down the hill, and both had moved over to stand behind a cluster of trees.

"Ohhhhh, I hope you can steer this thing or we'll go right in the creek." Sage laughed as they dropped down the smooth, snow-packed slope, picking up speed as the incline steepened.

"I'd better." Ross laughed in her ear, throwing his body to one side to angle their speeding conveyance.

"Ross . . . look out . . . steer the other way!" Sage shouted to him, caught between horror and laughter as she saw what was in front of them. It looked like a smooth ride that ended in a small valley to climb an incline again. Sage knew what looked like a wide swath up the other side of a hill was in reality a good five-foot drop-off, then a swing down a longer hill into the valley leading into the park. "Ohhh, Ross!" Sage squeezed her eyes shut as he misunderstood her consternation and threw his weight to the other side, steering them away from a stand of stunted pine.

"Don't worry, darling."

"Mo-therrr!" Tad called to them.

Pip stared at them wide-eyed.

"Uh-oh," Ross said in her ear, lifting her back against him so that she was hoisted into his lap when the toboggan was airborne.

They landed with a teeth-jolting jar, the momentum propelling them down the slope that had the look of a modified roller coaster.

"Hang on, darling!" Ross said, laughing in her ear.

They curved around more trees, then came to rest with a whoosh of snow against a pile of buried leaves.

"Great ride." Ross laughed aloud, wiping the puffs of snow from her cheeks.

"I was in the front catching all the spray." Amusement bubbled up in her as she looked at his face, which was encrusted with snow. "You look like Santa Claus, eyebrows, beard and all."

Ross kissed her nose. "So? I'll buy myself a red suit." He turned his head to watch as Pip and Tad ran up to them, out of breath.

"Ge-ee. Tha-at was good," Tad enthused, clapping his mittened hands.

Pip nodded, going up to Ross shyly when he held out his arms.

"Did you like it, too, cupcake?" He kissed the little girl, then pulled Tad down onto the toboggan, wrestling with him as he often did.

It made Sage catch her breath to see the sparkle in

Pip's eyes when she watched her brother and father. The little girl had made such strides since Ross's appearance in her life. It was such a marked change that even the neighbors had remarked on it.

They climbed the hill again with Ross pulling Pip on the toboggan and Sage pulling the other sled. Tad ran alongside, chattering at Ross nonstop.

Several more times they rode the hill, sometimes Ross with Tad or Pip. Sage would go with whomever was left.

When she saw Pip shiver, she signaled to Ross.

"Let's go, gang. Hot chocolate time, I think," Ross said, swinging the little girl up into his arms and carting her up the hill again, close to his body.

They put the sleds in the rack that a carpenter had made for them when Sage first decided to adopt the children, and then went into the house.

"I had forgotten how hot hot chocolate can be," Ross said, as the four of them sat on the floor in front of the fireplace. He put an ice cube in both Tad's and Pip's cups.

Sage chuckled, then handed him a thick slice of homemade wheat bread. She had made several loaves for the restaurant that morning. She saw the surprised look in his eye before he took the bread covered with peanut butter. "You like it now."

Ross nodded. "Strange but true." He grinned at her and offered her a bite of bread. "My tastebuds are going through change of life, and returning to childhood."

"There are sturgeons having apoplexy in the Caspian Sea at this moment," she said, smiling at him.

"I didn't say I'd given up eating caviar. I just said that I've developed a fondness for food that sticks to the roof of my mouth." Ross's fascinated gaze was fixed on the children as they took healthy bites of peanut butter and bread and followed them with sips of hot cocoa. "Good," he muttered, then lifted the bread to his mouth.

"Well?"

Ross kept chewing, rolling his eyes at her.

"Tell me."

"Give me a chance to unlock my jaws." Ross wiped his mouth on a napkin. "I like it." He finished the bread and cocoa. "I'll have some more," he told her, leaning across her lap and taking a bite from her bread. "Ummm. This tastes better."

"Pirate," Sage told him, trying to keep her voice from shaking when he snuggled his head into her lap.

"Yes," he told her smugly.

"Pla-ay ga-ame." Tad shook his father's sleeve.

"Okay," Ross agreed, sitting up and pulling Pip onto his lap. "Uncle Wiggly, here we come."

"You three play. I have to get my clothes ready for this evening."

Ross looked up, frowning. "You mean you were out there playing with us and you have to go to work tonight?"

Sage nodded.

"Get in that bedroom and take a nap."

"I can't, Ross. I have to iron—"

"I'll iron whatever's out there and I'll make their dinner too." He rose to his feet and turned her toward the bedroom. "Get some rest." He leaned closer to her. "I don't want you tired when you come home from the restaurant."

Sage could feel her ankles redden, then her knees, thighs, stomach, chest, neck, and face as she imagined the two of them in bed later that night. "Yessir," she cheeped.

"Sleep tight."

Sage was sure she would sleep because she hadn't slept that well the two nights that Ross had been gone. She lay down on the bed, staring up at the ceiling. "He's walked back into my life and put a noose around my neck," she said, sighing, her eyelids fluttering. "I thought I'd slipped loose, but it's tighter than it ever was." She turned over on her side and was asleep.

She woke and sat up all in one motion. Months with the children had taught her to trust her instincts. She had opened her eyes thinking that something or someone had fallen with an awful crash. It had happened! She was sure of it. She swung her feet to the floor just as the door opened.

"Darling, I'm sorry I woke you." Ross gave her a weak smile. "I dropped the iron." He shrugged. "I plugged it in again and it seems to be working. I left it on the counter to cool—"

"Too close to the edge," Sage finished for him, stifling a yawn. "I had a lovely nap."

Ross moved closer, gazing at her. "I fed the children and your cothes are ironed . . . and you look flushed and sensuous as hell."

She stretched her arms toward him in an unaccustomed gesture. "How odd. I look just the way I feel."

Ross closed his eyes a scant six inches from her. "Don't. Tad could come bounding in here any minute. Children certainly add a little raciness to an arrangement." He grinned at her ruefully when she laughed and rose to her feet.

She closed the small distance between them, slipping her arms around his waist. "Just think of all the character building you're doing."

"Taking ice-cold showers does not build character," he mumbled into her neck.

"Think positive."

"I am. Be ready to leave the restaurant on the dot. *No* chitchat tonight."

"Gotcha."

Ross tightened his hold on her. "You feel so good."

"So do you." Sage sighed, feeling more barriers crumble.

"Let's take a trip, just the two of us."

"When? Where?"

"As soon as possible. Name the place as long as it's private. I love the children, but I want to be alone with you."

"We leave for your parents' in two days . . . for Thanksgiving."

"Lord. I forgot."

"Maybe after the first of—"

Ross snapped his fingers, his brows furrowed in thought. "That's what we'll do. We'll stay at the gardener's cottage for two nights—"

"Gardener's cottage?"

"Yes. The one on the estate, you know, at the end of the drive that leads to the beach."

"But—I mean—it would take—"

"Not so," Ross interrupted again. "I took it over myself when you left. I used to go there on weekends—"

"With whom?" The words were out before Sage could control them.

Ross tapped her nose with his forefinger. "I was doing my hermit thing, lady."

"Hermit? You?"

"You don't know me as well as you thought you did."

"And you don't know me that well either."

"So? Let's try to work on that."

"Won't the children be staying with us?"

Ross shook his head. "We'll tell Mother she can have them for a few days"—he placed his finger over her lips when she opened her mouth to speak—"and we'll make sure that they hit it off first. I wouldn't leave Pip with anyone if she would be uncomfortable. You know that."

Sage thought of the little girl cuddled close to his chest as he read her a bedtime story. "Yes. I do know that."

"So what do you say?"

"Go for it!"

Ross hugged her. "My sentiments exactly."

Sage felt rather than heard a presence. She stretched to look over Ross's shoulder. "Pippa, darling, did you want Mommy?"

Pip nodded, going at once to Ross.

When he held out his arms she went into them with a big sigh, her fingers finding her mouth unerringly. "Daddy's going to make popcorn for his big girl tonight," Ross announced, smiling.

"Without butter," Sage admonished.

"Sans butter, sweet girlfriend."

"Smart guy." Sage wrinkled her nose at him, loving the way he looked at her.

By the time she left the three of them to go to work, Ross had made the popcorn in the air popper and was getting out the stack of books so the children might each choose a story to be read. Was she getting jealous? Did it bother her that Ross was not only good with them, but they sought out his company all the time?

It was a bit later than usual when Sage pulled into the driveway that night. And just as she did, the Ferrari was coming down the drive. When she paused, the sleek Italian sportscar reversed to the garage and stopped.

Ross was at her door even as she stopped, put her car in park, and turned off the motor. "I was worried."

"You were coming to get me?" Sage stepped down from the vehicle into his arms. "I wasn't that late."

"Late enough," he grated out, his fingers digging at her waist.

"Sorry."

"You should be." He breathed the words into her hair. It felt very good to hold her. "Why were you a little late?"

"I wore my Icelandic sweater tonight. You remember?

The one we bought when we took one of the Christmas trips to Gstaad?" She closed her eyes when he kissed her. "It . . . it made me recall that trip and I sat in the car a few minutes before driving home."

"The trip when you met Jorge."

"Yes." Sage felt his arm tighten at her waist as he turned her toward the house. "I was wondering how he and his wife were doing?"

"He's divorced . . . or in the process of being divorced." Ross had pepper in his tone. "The man isn't the type to be faithful to one woman."

"You know him well enough to make that judgment, do you?" Irritation laced Sage's voice.

"I think so," Ross riposted.

Sage shrugged. She didn't want to argue with Ross when things between them had been better than they had in years.

He turned her to face him. "I was jealous of him when we were in Reykjavik because he made you laugh. Then when he showed up in Gstaad the day I went to the top of the mountain with Slater"—Ross referred to his brother-in-law—"and I came down to find that you had gone skiing with him . . ." His mouth tightened.

Sage stared up at him. "He was willing to go on the intermediate trails with me."

"I would have gone with you."

"But you would have felt unfulfilled. You love the challenge of the seven-hour ski . . . of being airlifted in so that you could ski down. I would never be your peer in skiing . . . and, besides, I was too busy imagining you in an avalanche, or falling through a snow bridge or crevasse—"

"You never told me that you worried so."

"It would have been a burden to you."

Ross hauled in a deep breath, pressing his forehead to hers. "So." He pulled her closer. "And when we stayed on

Maui and I took part in the Iron Man. . . ." Ross referred to the grueling triathlon in Hawaii in which many of the strongest men buckled and couldn't finish. Ross had been in it three times and had always finished in the top hundred.

"That frightened me too." Sage laughed deprecatingly. "I had images of you drowning out there and no one helping you." Sage could feel the smile slipping off her face. She hadn't wanted to tell him that.

"I let you down," Ross told her. "I let you down because I didn't take into account your feelings." He brushed her hair back from her face.

"I should have spoken up. I contributed to my own pain. I shouldn't have walked away from you without telling you exactly how I felt."

"Right."

"Right." She laughed up at him.

While she was still chuckling, he leaned down and took her laughter into his mouth, her breath feathering through him. "Ummm, I like that."

"You do?"

"Oh, yes."

Sage felt a fluttery, flirtatious emotion dribbling through her. "Good for you." She bit the end of his nose lightly.

Ross felt a tingling down the back of his legs. He leaned over her, curtaining her with his body. "Shall we go in the house? It's cool here."

"Not too cool." Sage gave a breathy laugh.

Ross clamped her close to his side as they entered the house. "Did I ever tell you that you are a voluptuary?"

"I don't think so." Sage chuckled as together they managed to squeeze through the door leading from the garage.

"You are."

"You're one too."

Ross stopped in the hall of their bedroom wing. "Where you're concerned . . . yes, I am." He felt a rawness in his insides as though he had peeled back his flesh and let her see to the core of him. Years of masking his emotions, bobbing and weaving in all his relationships, had taught him how to hide, how to bury every facet of his behavior behind an impenetrable wall. It was a physical pain to let Sage see his vulnerability, but he knew that unless he hurt himself by lowering his guard, there was a chance he would lose her forever. If she once proceeded with the divorce, if neither of them backed down, then it would be over. Both of them had too much pride, both were too strong-willed—

"Where have you gone?"

Ross jerked himself out of his reverie and guided her into the bedroom. "I was thinking about us . . . about how it was going to hurt taking down the last barriers between us."

Sage nodded, facing him, her hands at her sides. She cleared her throat. "I think it's a distinct possibility that our marriage won't survive all this drilling of feelings." She gave a shaky laugh.

"That has to be the number-one priority then, that we take care of what we have and strengthen it and not allow any weakening."

"I feel like the boy with his finger in the dike."

Ross nodded. "A great deal rides on this, not only because of ourselves but because of the children too." He let his eyes rove her body from ankle to ear as he helped her out of her Icelandic sweater. "But you are definitely not a boy, Sage." He held the sweater in his hand for a moment, an arrested look in his eyes. "I remember how much I wanted to push Jorge off that mountain when you two came back that afternoon, laughing and joking. I felt excluded and didn't like it."

"I like Jorge. He's amusing."

"He felt more strongly about you."

Sage shook her head. "We were friends."

Ross kissed her hard. "I don't want to talk about anyone but ourselves."

"Good idea," Sage said softly, her eyes heavy-lidded and closing as he pulled the ribbed cotton sweater over her head, then kissed her again.

"I want to think of you and have you think of me." His words slurred against her skin as he bent over her.

"Uh-huh." Sage leaned against him as he slowly removed her bra and the gray woolen slacks that she wore, throwing all the clothing at the same chair, some of it missing and landing on the floor. She didn't care. Her mind was like melting wax. It couldn't hold a thought but that of Ross.

He lowered her onto the bed, then stripped the clothes from his body and followed her down. "I was worried about you when you didn't come home at the right time," he muttered into her breast.

"I didn't linger at the Gasthaus . . ." Her words fell from her lips as already her mind and body were on another planet with Ross.

"I waited five minutes past the time I judged you to be due home. Then I left the dog in the hall of the children's wing and went looking for you."

"The dog is a good guardian."

"Right."

Sage loved the warm abrasion of his muscular body on hers. She wriggled closer to him, wanting nothing more than his heat over her skin.

"Honey, that feels so good." Ross let his mouth slide from one breast to the other, taking hold of a nipple and beginning a tender massage of it with his tongue. Each pulling and suckling motion had her body arching under him. "Not yet, love."

"Yes, please."

"You're so polite." Ross choked back a laugh.

He pressed her down to the bed with his hands, holding her gently while he slowly traveled her skin with his lips. When his mouth entered her in the most intimate joining, her ragged cry made his own libido jump through his skin.

"No more."

"All right, darling." Ross's voice hoarsened with his want of her.

He positioned himself over her with great care, as he always had, even after years of marriage, wary of giving her discomfort. He entered her with a gentle violence that had her body rocking with building passion. "Angel," Ross croaked out as her form imprisoned him.

"Ross," Sage wailed as she clung to him.

They scaled the peaks where only lovers go, and soared in the most blissful but torrid togetherness.

Long moments after their climax they stayed together, holding each other, clinging as though if they parted, life would seep away.

"Ross . . ."

"Yes." His voice was muffled in her hair.

"I know this isn't all of marriage, nor all of life, but it is a beautiful part, isn't it?"

"With us it is, yes."

"It's important to show love this way," Sage murmured.

"Very."

She wriggled to get comfortable, not releasing the hold she had on his waist.

"Don't do that. We'll be starting up again."

She giggled.

"Don't you believe me?"

"I think you're bragging."

Ross flipped her over onto his chest, so that her long blond hair fell around them. "You think that, do you?"

Sage laughed aloud and nodded, loving the feel of his hand massaging her body.

Ross slid her down further, so that she could feel his arousal. "And what do you call that?"

Sage chuckled. "Not chopped liver."

"Brat." Ross patted her behind and clamped her close to him. "Pay the price."

"What price?"

"The price of not knowing when it was time to make love."

"How much?"

He shrugged, then slowly fitted her body to his, keeping her over him. "Priceless," he choked out.

"Yes."

Even as they made slow, sweet love again, the cold thought of how Sage might be when they returned to Long Island flitted across his brain. He blotted it from his mind and let passion take him away.

Nine

When the limousine that had picked them up at the airport slid into the turn at the wide gates, Sage felt her heart sink, then beat out of rhythm. She had returned to Highgate! She swallowed painfully knowing that if it weren't snowing so hard, she would be able to see Ross's and her home a little more than a mile from his parents' home. When they passed the gardener's cottage, Sage glanced at Ross and found him looking at her.

"Yes. That's where I went through so much thinking about us, Sage."

"It was always a pretty place," Sage responded conversationally, her insides shredding.

"Mom-my. It-t's big." Tad knelt on the front seat and turned to tell them.

Pip nodded and pushed closer to Ross. "Big," she whispered.

Sage and Ross stared at the child, then at each other.

Ross kissed Pip. "She's not nervous, anyway." Ross gave a rough laugh when Sage's lips tightened. Then he lifted the little girl into his lap. "Daddy is proud of his girl."

With a slight skid the car came to a stop under the cement portico that gave some shelter from the storm. Even as the chauffeur, Hudgins, got out of the car and opened the back door, the door to the house was thrown open and Mr. and Mrs. Joshua Tempest were standing there, coats thrown over their shoulders.

"Hurry, Hudgins. Get the children in here." Though diminutive and with a low voice, Hepzibah Tempest was always heard. "Stephens, please go out and help Hudgins."

Sage knew she was talking to the butler, who had been with them since Ross had been a baby. She took a deep breath and slid across the plush upholstery to take the hand Ross held out to her. He already had Pip high in his arms and Tad danced around him with a mixture of excitement and curiosity. Sage looked at her son and wished she had one-quarter of his panache at this moment. She took his hand and climbed the fan-shaped cement steps that led to the front door. "Hello, Heppie, sir." Sage spoke in the stilted way she had always used with her in-laws. When she saw her mother-in-law bite her lip and step back, and the flash of hurt on her father-in-law's face, she realized once more how often she had been cold with them. She forced a smile to her lips. "It's lovely to be at Highgate for Thanksgiving."

Her father-in-law sighed and nodded his head, then moved forward to embrace her. "It's good to have you here."

Sage hugged him back, feeling a sting of tears. She felt the smile tremble off her face.

"You're a good girl, Sage," Joshua St. John Tempest told his daughter-in-law.

Sage pulled back, hesitating for a moment, then went to hug her mother-in-law, something she had never done.

Heppie gripped her arms. "My dear . . . my dear." Her voice broke and she coughed. "But the children, we must close the door so they won't freeze." She looked at Tad. "My goodness, what a big boy you are. Your father was just like that at your age."

The arrested look on Tad's face told Sage that he had been suddenly reminded of his own father. Then his face cleared. "You me-an Ro-ss, our da-ddy now." Tad beamed and put out his hand.

Heppie glowed, took his hand, then kissed him, leaning back to speak so that he could read her lips. "Yes, dear. I meant that, but I amend it. Your manners are better than your father's."

"Never," Ross told his mother, then leaned down to kiss her cheek, his insides melting in delight at how the day had begun. He couldn't recall a time that Sage and his parents had ever exchanged an embrace. Their meetings were always cordial but cautious. It would be nice if they could be good friends, but he knew that it didn't matter if his parents hated Sage. He wanted her in his life, and he was going to get her and keep her!

"Sinjon, why were you looking so grim when I kissed you?" his mother asked testily. "One would think I made you uncomfortable."

Ross shot a quick glance at his perceptive parent. "Not so, Mother. I was just wondering if I should ask Shakeley to make the children some cocoa."

His mother shook her head and grimaced. "I wish you could ask Shakeley that. The poor dear fell two weeks ago and broke her ankle. She's recuperating at her sister's. Her two nieces were here until yesterday but they had to go home for Thanksgiving, so we're waiting for the people from Gourmet, Incorporated, to send kitchen staff."

"It looks bad out there, Mother. I hope they get through," Ross told her.

"They must." Heppie shepherded the children across the spacious marble two-story foyer with its sparkling crystal chandelier through double oak doors into another very large room done in pinks, greens, and blues to pick up the colors in the Kerman rugs on the floor.

Sage had always liked the living room and had done her own living room at Wayside, her and Ross's house in the country, in shades of pale green, cream, and pink to match their rugs. She looked around her and smiled at her father-in-law when she caught him watching her.

He ambled to her side. "It is good to have you here, child. We've missed you."

She put her hand through his arm and reached up and kissed him. "I didn't realize until now how much I missed all of you."

Ross shot a quick look at his father and Sage before looking back at his worried mother. "For heaven's sake, Mother, you must have guessed that your hired help might not get here just by looking out a window. We are your only guests that made it—"

"Don't be ridiculous," Heppie interrupted, frowning up at her son. "Everyone is here. Some have gone out cross-country skiing, some are down at the pool, and the others are playing tennis or racquetball, I suppose." She flapped a hand at him as though what she had told him was of no importance. "What shall I do if they don't get here? We have a cocktail party this evening and the buffet, which is not difficult. We could even serve it ourselves, but what about tomorrow? If no one comes? No, no, I will not dwell on such a happening. It would be too awful. They will be here as soon as the weather lets up."

"And if it doesn't?" Ross helped Pip to the crackers and cheeses on the coffee table in front of the fireplace, then poured her some cider, his mind not on what he was doing. Was he right in suspecting that his mother had filled the house with guests for the holiday? Dammit, Sage was having enough problems with this reunion without facing a brace of strangers. "Mother, who is here? Besides the family, I mean."

"Just the family. Your sisters and their families . . . oh, of course, Jorge Mendez. I invited him because he's such a good friend of Sage's and with his recent divorce he was rather at loose ends."

Ross felt his face freeze. "I see."

"Is something bothering you, Sinjon?"

"No." Ross moved toward the children.

Tad, who never needed a second invitation to partake of food, was munching happily on crackers and cheese and wedges of apple, which he was washing down with drinks of cider. "Thi-is is good. Have some?" he offered his father, who smiled at him vaguely and shook his head.

"And how is the Norcross venture doing, Ross?" Joshua patted his son on the back, then hunkered down in front of Tad and Pip.

"Ah . . . fine." Ross looked at Sage, who had a puzzled look on her face.

"You said that Norcross was a thorn in your side."

"Did I say that, darling?" Ross rose to his feet and pulled Sage into his arms and kissed her hard on the mouth. "I forgot."

Joshua guffawed.

"I certainly hope you don't do that all the time in front of the children," his mother said, tight-lipped.

"Why not? We used to." Joshua patted her back and kissed her on the forehead.

"We did not." Heppie pushed at his chest, but she

couldn't mask the smile when she looked at her husband. "Come and sit down and we'll have tea while the children are snacking and while Stephens takes the luggage to the rooms." She patted the seat next to her on the settee. "Sit here, Sage, and tell me about the German restaurant you own."

"That I own with my partner, Gusti Baumann. We met when I was an exchange student in Germany and we kept in touch. When he and his family decided to settle in upstate New York, I visited with them whenever I stayed with my aunt. He married an upstater." She smiled at her mother-in-law, not feeling as stiff with her as she had at other times. "We often discussed German food and how there were no restaurants in the area that served the wonderful recipes that we enjoyed."

"So, you went ahead and started one with your friend," Joshua finished for her.

"Something like that, with a few pitfalls along the way."

"I've been doing the books for the Gasthaus and they have been consistently in the black for the last three months," Ross offered.

"You! The president of Worldwide Temp Industries doing books!" His mother's mouth sagged.

His father laughed. "Wonderful. I thought you might have forgotten how."

Ross gave his father a tight grin. "Did you think I was getting soft?"

"Must have been. You let Sage get away."

Ross's teeth came together with a crack.

"Stop it, you two." Heppie shot an irritated look at her husband. "Sage, here's Stephens to take you to your rooms."

Sage saw the stiff set of Ross's shoulders before she rose and took hold of Pip's hand. She left the room, knowing Ross was fuming and quite sure he was right behind her with Tad.

Pip's hand tightened on Sage's as they traveled up the curving staircase to the second floor, then up a wide split staircase to the third floor, where Stephens led them into the blue wing.

"Ni-ice."

"Glad you like it." Ross grinned at the boy as he bounced on the bed. "I had this room once." He led the children through to the other, smaller room that would be Pip's. "And this was where I used to study—at least that's what I was supposed to do."

Pip was goggle-eyed when she saw the pink-and-white-eyelet bedroom with the canopy bed and the two Cabbage Patch dolls seated at an oak table and chair set.

"My goodness," Sage whispered. "And I was thinking of trying to get her one for Christmas."

"Don't ask me how Mother manages the impossible. I don't know." There was acid in Ross's voice. He wished they hadn't come. For two pins he would pack Sage and the children up and take them home to Irondequoit, snow or no snow.

The little girl grasped the two dolls and hugged them to her, her eyes closed in ecstasy.

Ross and Sage watched her in silence.

"Pi-p li-kes her dol-ls," Tad told them.

"Indeed she does." Ross's voice was laced with amusement. His arm slid around Sage's waist. "Before you tell me you hate it here and you wish we hadn't come, let me tell you I agree with you."

Sage opened her mouth to tell him that she didn't hate it at Highgate.

He caught her lips with his in a hard kiss before she spoke, then released her and spun away. "I'll be in our room down the hall. I want to make a few calls."

Sage stared at the wall, her mind and spirit in turmoil.

"I like it he-re," Tad announced with his usual verve.

Pip, standing close to Tad, nodded, the large eyes she turned up to her mother warm and sparkling.

Sage bent down in front of the two of them, touching one of the dolls. "And you like the Cabbage Patch kids."

Pip nodded again as a knock sounded at the door.

Stephens entered, smiling at the children. "I've come to get Tad and Pip, Mrs. Tempest, to take them down to the pool." His lips lifted a little when he saw her sudden frown. "Not to worry, madame. One of the family is acting as lifeguard." He coughed. "And, as you know, in my youth, I swam for Great Britain."

Sage nodded, smiling as the children jumped around her, begging to get into their bathing suits.

After they left, each holding one of Stephens's hands, Sage turned to unpack their clothes.

"I'll do that, madame. I'm Elsie."

Sage smiled at the maid and thanked her, then went down the hall to the suite that she and Ross would share. He was nowhere to be found, so she assumed he had gone down to the gym located in the huge basement level of the house. Her father-in-law had been a great athlete in his day, winning a bronze medal in the Olympics for running, and had renovated the house from top to bottom when he had taken over from his father. He had poured a fortune into the basement gymnasium, determined that his son and daughters would be into physical fitness.

"And they are," Sage murmured to herself as she donned a sweatsuit and sneakers and put bathing suit, cap, and goggles into a small carryall. She would swim with the children while Ross played racquetball. Maybe they would even play tennis later on in the bubble-covered court that was adjacent to the pool.

Walking on the plush carpeting down the spacious halls, she knew that if she stretched her arms wide she still wouldn't be able to touch the oak wainscoted walls. Familiarity brought a flood of memories of the times she had stayed here when she and Ross were engaged. Laughter had been the order of the day. Love had been the very essence of their existence. They hadn't been able to walk down a hall without kissing or touching. She had been dazed by the monumental feeling engendered by Ross, transported by joy because Ross St. John Tempest thought she was beautiful!

Sage shook her head, not wanting to think of that young and foolish girl who really believed that all her dreams would come true the day she became his wife.

She found she hadn't forgotten her way in that great pile of a house. She only made one wrong turn in the maze of corridors. She glanced in the window of the racquetball courts where Ross was playing with his brother-in-law Slater Caldwell, who belonged to the law firm of Caldwell, Rivers, and Dean, the firm that represented Worldwide Temp. Ross was too intent on his point to notice her. Then she was past and walking through the steel door that led up a ramp to the short covered walk to the pool and indoor tennis court. It was a little cooler in the short tunnel and she shivered, happy to enter the hot, steamy air of the pool.

"Mom-my, wat-ch me," Tad called from the far end, where he was poised on the diving board.

Sage knew there were others there calling to her, but she kept her eyes riveted to her son, knowing he was more than capable of diving from the diving board, but still harboring a trace of trepidation when she saw him bounce once and do a rather leg-tangled jackknife dive without too much splash. Sage clapped, feeling her face stretch in a proud smile. When Pip followed him off the board in a straight dive, she thought her heart would burst. She became aware that others were applauding her children's efforts and turned to look at a cluster of Ross's family seated around the pool.

"If they are as intrepid on the tennis court as they are in the water, I can see tough competition."

"Jorge!" Sage forgot about Ross's sisters, Barbara and Leslie, who were calling to her, in the excitement of seeing her old friend. "How are you?" Sage bit her lip. "What a stupid question! I'm sorry about your . . . your marriage."

Jorge shrugged. "Don't be. I'm not. I understand that you've filed for divorce." Jorge's dark eyes danced over her. "That's good news." His voice lowered so that the others wouldn't hear him. "Don't tell me I'm wrong. I don't want to hear it." He took her arm. "Come on. It's time to face the Golden Herd."

Sage laughed aloud. Jorge had always referred to Ross's family that way and it always made her laugh.

Someone took her arm and turned her away from Jorge. "Time to say hello to the family, sister-in-law."

Sage spun around and looked up the lanky length of her brother-in-law Barry Ditwell, who was married to Ross's sister Barbara. "Barry. How are you?" Sage put out her hand.

Barry ignored her hand and caught her in a bear hug, his thin body surprisingly strong. "No handshakes, lady. I've missed you. Outside of my wife, you're the only one I can stand in this pride of lions." His lopsided grin touched her, then disappeared. "Truth. We have missed you."

"Thank you."

"You have great kids. I told Barb we are getting Will and Debbie into a swim program after seeing your two."

"That's what he said." The lazy voice came from Sage's blind side but she recognized the voice.

"Barbara, how are you?" Sage turned and stared at

her sister-in-law, who was as tall as she. She had always had a wary rather than a warm relationship with Ross's sibling. Barbara was outspoken and self-confident like all the Tempests, and she didn't suffer fools gladly.

"Fine. Are you back to stay or visit?"

"Babs!"

"Well, I was just asking."

"When I know the answer, I'll tell you," Sage answered casually, feeling relaxed all at once and in charge of herself.

"Touché."

"Clever repartee, Barry," his wife snapped, eliciting a delighted laugh from him.

"I've been waiting a long time to see Sage score off this group. What about you, Jorge?"

Jorge chuckled, leaning over and kissing Sage. "I always knew she would be able to handle herself if she ever made up her mind."

"Have I missed something?" Ross stood near the doorway leading from the pool to the gym, his hair plastered to his forehead, perspiration glinting on his face, his racquet clutched in his hand like a club.

Sage felt his fury vibrating across the space separating them and lifted her chin. Instinct told her it was because Jorge had kissed her. Amusement vied with irritation. Hadn't she been the possessive one? The insecure one? Now she could see that same acid fury on Ross's face that she often felt. Had he always been like that but she had been too buried in her own feelings to notice? When she had flirted lightly at Bending Bough Country Club, it hadn't seemed to bother him. She felt a reckless anger with Ross and herself. Why had they been so stupid with one another? "You don't generally miss much," she drawled, noting the heads whipping her way as her husband seemed to exhale phosphorous.

"I try not to." Ross spat the words.

"Hooray for you." Sage turned her back on him and heard her husband's indrawn breath and Barry's low whistle.

"Mom-my. Co-me swim-ming."

"Coming, Tad." She went into one of the dressing rooms lining the wall and changed into the pale blue one-piece Lycra that was slashed high on each thigh and plunged almost to her coccyx in the back. She studied herself in the wall mirror. She was thinner but her breasts and backside were still quite rounded. Her legs looked even longer than they did when she weighed much more. She shrugged at her image, grabbed her cap and goggles, and left the cubicle.

She looked neither right nor left, but kept her eyes on Pip and Tad, who had made friends with some of Ross's nephews and nieces and were now playing a game. "Hey. Who's for water polo?"

Pip swam to her brother and poked his hand, signing what Sage had just said to the other children.

"Ye-es, Mommy. We-e play!" Tad shouted in his dissonant voice, making many of the adults sitting around the pool chortle at his enthusiasm.

"He's a wonderful boy. Hearing-impaired, isn't he?" Jorge said at her side.

"Yes, but he lip-reads beautifully and he's very bright." Sage couldn't keep the pride from her voice. "Excuse me, Jorge. Water polo is calling."

"I'll join you. I used to play myself."

Sage took note of the rather brief swimsuit he had donned and nodded. She dove from the side of the pool, keeping well away from the children as she entered the water, then swimming to them under the surface. "Hi," she gasped, laughing as she came up next to Pip.

"Hi."

"Oh, Pip, darling. You're talking more and more."

Jorge was there, sweeping his dark hair from his eyes.

"I understood she was a mute, but that was a very clear sound I heard." He laughed and chucked the little girl under the chin.

Sage could tell that behind the shy confusion Pip was delighted with what Jorge had said. "Come over here," she called out to all the children. Though they weren't as fast and sure in the water as Tad and Pip, they were eager and able enough.

Tad and Will, Barbara's boy who was a year older than Tad, were picked as captains. Then the sides had to be chosen.

Sage made a face when Jorge was chosen first by Will. Then she looked past him to the poolside, where Ross, now in a swimsuit, stood next to Barry.

They both entered the water in clean dives.

Sage was treading water in the deep end of the pool when she felt the tug on her ankle. Down she went, managing to gulp some air before the water closed over her head.

Ross thought the water would start steaming in a second, he felt such ire with her, and no amount of reason entered into it. Then he yanked her close to him and breathed what air he had into her mouth.

She popped up to the surface again, breathing hard and ready to do mayhem to him. When she saw Pip and Tad paddling through the water toward her, laughing, she satisfied herself with a glare.

"Do your worst, lady," Ross dared her, his teeth glinting in a crocodile smile.

Sage flathanded water at him. "I'm playing water polo."

"So are we." Barry splashed up to them in an awkward crawl. "I'm on your team, Ross. Sage is on with Jorge."

"No!" Ross roared, effectively silencing all the chitchat of the pool-siders.

"Don't be more a fool than you can help." Sage treaded water and lambasted her husband.

"Don't speak to me like that."

"Then stop roaring like a lion. The children are watching you."

Ross's mouth opened and closed. Then his gaze swept over the cluster of boys and girls in the shallow end, including Pip and Tad, who had joined the others. He threw his body sideways in a racing dive and went to join Barry now at the side of the pool.

Sage saw the sour twist of a smile on Ross's face as the play began, and she watched him warily. When she saw him hold Pip up in the air so that the little girl could throw the ball, she exhaled in relief. Perhaps he had cooled down. She hoped so.

One by one Ross's other relatives changed into swimsuits and joined the fray in the pool. All the Tempests were fierce competitors, even down to the children, so that the challenge smoked the pool once they were all in it.

Sage drove upward to take the ball away from Barry, laughing when she heard him shout in protest. When she went to throw it, two hands gripped her waist, lifting her and tossing her upward. Reaction made her release the ball. She recognized the hard laugh behind her and knew that Ross was still in white fury and not all the pool water in the world would cool him down.

The game escalated, the laughter and shouts threatening to make the walls of the pool tremble.

Ross watched Sage after he threw her into the air, a bedrock satisfaction in him that he had disconcerted her. He saw Jorge with the ball and shot past the other players to engage him one-on-one. Dueling, bobbing, and weaving, the two men fought for the ball, both sides cheering on their gladiators.

"Gotcha." Jorge's teeth gleamed triumphantly as he whisked the ball from Ross again.

"Not yet." Ross went up and right over the top of him, taking the ball and throwing it in one powerful swoop toward the netted hoop at the far end of the pool. With a swish and rousing cheers it went in and the game was over.

Ross arrowed his way to Sage's side, not taking note of his teammates, who congratulated him and themselves while jeering at the opposition. "See, love, I always win."

"Turn blue." Sage slapped water at him and swam to the side. Before she could lever herself out, she was lifted up and onto the carpeted surround. "Thanks," she said huffily, Ross's rough laugh making the tiny hairs on her body stand straight out.

Every head turned when the pool door crashed open and Heppie Tempest stood there wringing her hands, her husband trying to calm her. "Oh dear, oh dear. We have no one to cook Thanksgiving dinner. The cook and kitchen help can't make it through the storm."

Ten

Sage looked at her mother-in-law and saw how her hands were shaking and her eyes shining with tears. "Don't worry, Heppie. Cooking is my business. We'll have a wonderful dinner tomorrow. Just let me get dressed." Sage heard Ross's negative expletive at the same time Heppie moaned. "Lord, we could get poisoned."

Sage dressed, alternately cursing and laughing. Damn this family! They said anything that came into their heads. How many times had her feelings been lacerated by the outspoken, thick-skinned Tempest crew? Goodness, she couldn't count the times. It surprised her that even her mother-in-law's remark hadn't bothered her too much. She shrugged. That's what having Pip and Tad had done for her. Mothers were a tough breed. She grinned at herself in the cubicle mirror after taking a shower and shampooing her hair to get the chlorine out of it.

She returned to the pool area, surprised to find Ross coming out of a cubicle with Tad, then going into the one next door and getting Pip, whose hair was brushed and whose pink corded jeans and matching shirt looked fresh and neat. She had forgotten about both children in her agitation with the Tempest family! Foremost, the oldest son!

Jorge approached her. "Sage, darling, I can help you. I'm considered a good cook among my friends."

"Women, of course."

Jorge's devilish grin acknowledged the truth of that.

Heppie rounded the pool, her high heels seeming incongruous in the steamy atmosphere of the pool area. "Ah . . . Sage, dear. I'm sure you're very good at German food, but Thanksgiving isn't German—"

"Not to worry, Mother. Sage knows all about turkeys. She keeps a wild one in her yard," Ross drawled, glancing at the children as they left the pool bubble to go through to the gymnasium. Tad called out they were going off to play Ping-Pong.

"She's . . . going . . . to . . . wring . . . its neck . . . for . . . dinner?" Heppie asked in fading accents.

"Morris is not for cooking," Sage riposted tartly, giving Ross a murderous look.

"She calls the turkeys by name, Joshua." Heppie rolled her eyes at her husband.

"Quaint custom." Joshua's eyes twinkled when Sage gave him an exasperated look.

"Morris is a wild turkey who lives in the park adjoining our property. He is a pet to most of the children there."

"Heavens. I hadn't realized how primitive it was in the western part of the state."

Sage's lips tightened when Ross gave a bark of laughter.

"Ahem." Barbara glided up to them. "Leslie and I will help you, Sage. I make a fabulous fondue and Les is marvelous with pâté."

"The turkey will be delighted," Jorge observed, earning a grateful grin from Sage and a glower from Ross.

After checking on the children in the gymnasium, Sage led the family contingent toward the house proper. She inhaled with delight on entering the monstrous chrome-and-oak kitchen. It was the equal in size of the Gasthaus's and it would be hers for two days. She looked lovingly at the scores of copper and steel pans and utensils that hung from racks above the huge work area. There were two sets of sinks in strategic places plus a small vegetable sink on the work table. "Pie baking first," she said, going to a closed section of counter and cupboard that when opened up revealed a pastry board and all accoutrements for baking.

"How do we start?" Barbara wrinkled her nose.

"Put on an apron." Sage flung open a floor-to-ceiling kitchen linen closet. "You and Les"—Sage referred to Ross's younger sister—"can make the pies. I'll give you step-by-step on the recipes. Slater, you can peel and slice the apples. Barry, you can mix the pumpkin." Sage turned and faced Ross's family and had to swallow laughter. Their mouths were hanging open. "Well?"

"What does Ross do?" Slater fumbled with his apron strings and glared at his grinning brother-in-law.

"I will see to the wine—"

"And you will see that the children set the table, but you can also put out the crystal. Under your mother's direction, of course." Sage raised her chin when she saw him bare his teeth.

"Of course." He inclined his head in sulfurous courtesy.

"I'll help with that. Ross is a novice at housework," Joshua said mildly, biting his lip in amusement when his son rounded on him.

The children clattered into the kitchen and Sage had to choke down a laugh when they all announced they would help Uncle Ross and Grampa.

"I he-lp," Tad thundered, after his sister signed what Sage had said.

For a fraction of a second Ross felt like the fox being cornered by the hounds. Damn you, Sage! He saw her watching him, trying not to laugh. "Let's go, gang. Grandpa will show us where everything is."

Stephens coughed from the doorway "Perhaps I can help you, sir, and Elsie will give a hand when she finishes her cleaning."

When the door closed behind them, Sage gave staccato directions to the pie group, then turned to take the two huge turkeys out of the walk-in refrigerator/freezer built into the wall of the butler's pantry. She sighed in delight as she looked at the plump, full-breasted fowl.

"Not to worry, dear. I shall help you." Heppie gave a nervous titter. "Just tell me what to do."

Sage nodded and did just that. "I need cornmeal to make corn bread . . ." she began.

Conversation fell to a buzz of necessary words as the Tempests began what was for them a novel experience.

Several hours later, Sage looked around her. The apple pies were cooling. All the dry ingredients were mixed and set aside for stuffing, the giblets were cooked for gravy, the fresh cranberry jelly prepared.

"How do the pies look?" Barbara asked, her voice tinged with both pride and trepidation.

"Good." Sage walked along the room checking every item on the counter, taking little notice when Ross, his father, and the children entered the kitchen and stood quietly watching her. "Good," she repeated to herself. "We roll tomorrow at eight o'clock sharp," she said abruptly, looking at each one in turn.

"Right you are, Guv," Barry saluted, making her laugh.

Ross inclined his head, watching her but saying nothing as the others plied her with questions. No wonder she was making a success of her business, he thought. She was efficient and she left nothing to chance. He ran a lazy glance around the kitchen and took note that much of the untidiness that went along with preparing a meal was taken care of as each step in the work was completed. She had the soul of a field marshal when it came to her work. A flash of fear laced his amusement. He had a warp-speed vision of her rising to the top of the restaurant business and walking away from him. His insides twisted in rejection of it. His indolent stance against the wall belied his inner turmoil. Damn her, she wasn't getting away from him. And he damn well wasn't going to be separated from his own children!

"It's a good thing Sage is here," his father said blandly. "Your mother feels far more relaxed now. I can tell."

"Super."

"A bit edgy, aren't you?"

"Am I?"

"Yes, I think so." His father coughed delicately behind his hand. "She's well organized and confident. Who would have thought our shy little Sage would bloom into a tiger lily?"

"Quite a poet, aren't you?"

"Ah . . . perhaps. It's such a relief to know your mother won't be in a swivet about the dinner tomorrow."

"Terrific." Ross felt his whole body freeze over when

his father chuckled. He shouldn't have brought her here! She hadn't wanted to come!

"And tonight, Sage . . . ?" Heppie brought her list of foods and menu for the buffet that evening to her daughter-in-law.

Sage took the papers and scanned them silently for a moment, then looked up, wondering at the quiet. The Tempest clan was watching her. She felt an uncomfortable redness reaching from her toes to her neck! She looked down at the papers again, the writing dancing in front of her eyes. "Fine."

"Does that mean we serve ourselves, dear? Isn't there anything we have to do first?"

"Why not leave Sage alone for now, Mother? She and I will go over the lists when we're changing." Ross pushed off the wall and went to his wife's side, slipping one arm around her and taking the papers from her hand with the other. When she turned to look up at him, a dazed expression on her face, he kissed her full on the lips.

"Dad-dy does tha-at all the ti-ime," Tad casually informed the assemblage.

"Does he now?" Slater looked at his brother-in-law and chortled. "Hoist with your own . . . ahem, petard, as they say?"

Ross looked at him without comment.

"Well, then . . ." Heppie folded her hands in front of her. "Perhaps you and I could meet here"—she looked at Sage and spread one hand to encompass the kitchen—"at say, four—"

"Make it five," her son interrupted.

"Really, Sinjon—"

"Five, Mother . . . and Stephens informs me that the gardener's cottage is ready for us, so Sage and I will be spending Thanksgiving night and the next day there."

Heppie put her arm around Pip's shoulders, hugging

the little girl. "Not with the children, I trust. I've hardly had a chance to talk to them."

Ross looked at the little girl and smiled. "If Tad and Pip wish to stay in the big house, they may, but if they want to come with us, they can do that too. There are three bedrooms down there." Ross smiled at Sage when he saw her exhale with relief.

"Time for the children to nap, I think, Heppie." Joshua narrowed his gaze on some of the children, then fixed it on Sage and Ross, a quizzical smile playing over his mouth. "We'll let Sage drag her kill to her lair." He barked a laugh when his family stared at him in puzzlement and his son grimaced at him.

Sage herded the children ahead of her, noting that Pip was yawning. "Come along. You can sleep before the supper hour."

"I'll take them, madame. Mr. Joshua said we were to take care of them and help you tomorrow too." Elsie grinned at the children. "We have plenty of help . . . just no cook. The missus almost had a cow." She laughed, then took a hand of Pip and Tad and preceded Sage up the stairs.

"My mother would have loved that description of herself," Ross said at her back, kissing her nape.

Sage hurried up the stairs.

"Damn it all that you are cooking for this large group." Ross caught up with her on the third-floor corridor.

"I don't mind. After all, that is my profession."

"If that's a shot at me—inferring that I don't think you have a very important position . . ."

Sage stopped walking and gaped at him. "Are you off your loaf? I never thought such a thing. Is that what you've been thinking all along? That my being a restauratrice was unimportant? Because if it is—"

"Dammit, Sage." Ross took hold of her upper arms, his face a mask of frustration. "No more."

She gulped, her mouth opening and closing.

"Truce?" He brushed his mouth over hers, feeling his heart tempo double. "It's Thanksgiving."

She nodded. "About going down to the gardener's cottage—"

He placed his index finger over her lips. "Just overnight if it makes you uncomfortable. One night should be all right. Yes?"

"Yes."

"Speak up, lady, I can barely hear you." Ross pulled her closer, relief making the blood flow back to his extremities.

"Yes." She nipped his neck with her teeth.

"Ouch." The bite stung him into arousal. "Lord, we had better get out of this hallway."

"Ross!" Sage looked at him, half-laughing, half-horrified.

He pressed her close to him. "See what you do to me."

Delighted, she wriggled slowly. "My, my. Shall I sit on your lap?"

Surprise held him still. "Yes." She hadn't been playful with him in a long time. "Let's take a nap."

"Tired?"

"It's a euphemism in this case."

"The children might come in."

"Elsie is with them."

Sage felt weak and responsive.

"Say yes."

Sage nodded.

Ross smiled and put his arm around her, and led her toward the master bedroom of the wing of the house assigned to them.

As they entered the bedroom, the small light on the phone was winking.

"Lord, a phone call, or one of the family wants to talk forever." Ross released her so suddenly she almost stumbled. He didn't notice. He was charging at the phone like a rampaging steer. "What? No. Absolutely not. She'll be down after we've rested. No, she is not coming to the phone, Barbara, and don't put Leslie on either. Yes, I know I'm the reincarnation of Genghis Khan. Good-bye." Ross slammed down the receiver, then pressed a button on the console to hold all calls.

Sage stared at him, her bottom lip clenched in her teeth, wanting to laugh aloud at the fierce little-boy look on her husband's face.

He stomped back to her, leaned down, and gave her a hard, searching kiss on the mouth. "Be right back." He left the room almost without breaking stride.

Sage blinked at the spot where he had been in the open doorway. She could hear him mumbling to himself, then a door slamming and a bolt being pushed into a lock. He sounded as though he were running when he returned.

"Hi." Ross stood in the doorway, a slow smile on his face. "I locked the door of the suite."

Sage smiled back as he walked to her.

He leaned down and nibbled on her lower lip, then pulled her sweatshirt up and over her head. "Does this suit you?"

"What?" Sage smiled at him dazedly as he sat her down on the bed and eased the sweatpants down to her ankles.

"That we make love now."

"Good idea." Sage was sure she was hyperventilating.

"I think so." Ross swung her hips around so she was lying on the bed, then dropped down next to her. "Warm enough?" He pulled the quilt over the two of them.

"Very warm day." Sage swiped at the perspiration on her upper lip.

"Snowing out. Windchill well below zero." He nuzzled

between her breasts, his warm breath feathering over her in erotic massage.

" 'Zat so?" The words bubbled out of her.

"Yes." Ross's tongue caressed the soles of her feet. Her quivering body was setting him on fire.

Sage felt the tremor in his hand as he continued to caress her, and passion gushed in her like a flash flood. "Ross . . ." She wanted to explain that it shouldn't be like this, that they should talk about their life more, not just allow the torrent of emotion to take them when it would. Life isn't like this, she wanted to tell him. The practical side of life doesn't allow for continual forays into a sexual world with no account of day-to-day living.

All the good reasons for forgoing love were there, but she spoke none of them, becoming the slave of her feelings for Ross before she could articulate.

"Come with me, love," he crooned to her. "Where no one else can go, just the two of us."

"Yes." She clutched him, her long legs manacling her to his body when he entered her.

The universe exploded, mushrooming her up and away from earth. All the mundane reasons to be practical fragmented around them.

Sage heard tiny moans of delight and knew they were hers. "That was lovely," she told Ross without opening her eyes, yet knowing he leaned over her,

"You liked that, did you?" he asked hoarsely.

She nodded, eyes still shut, lifting a hand to pat his cheek. "You're better at this than you are at making a living . . . and I know you're very good at that."

Ross stiffened for a moment, thinking she was jabbing at him about the many nights he'd left her alone and gone to business dinners . . . sometimes even seminars that would last for days.

Her eyes flickered open and fixed on him. "What's wrong?"

"Nothing, sweetheart." He buried his face in her hair. He didn't give a damn if she was zinging him, he wasn't going to upset the beautiful thing between them by asking her. "I like staring at your body."

"Indulge yourself."

"Wanton."

She looked thoughtful. "I think I must be." She squinted up at him. "Do you suppose it's change of life?"

Ross felt another stab. Didn't she recall that they had always been like this . . . in the beginning of their marriage? "Could be, but you are a little young for it."

"True." She snuggled closer to him. "You are so warm."

They were face-to-face, body to body.

Ross could feel his blood pressure rise. He felt as though he'd just hotdogged off Mount Everest on skis.

The bang on the door and subsequent calling brought Sage to a sitting position. "Tad."

Ross grimaced. "I love our son, but his timing is poor."

Sage chuckled and tickled him on the stomach, the feel of the hard, flat flesh a tingling stimulation to her senses.

"Keep that up and I'll tell Elsie to take them outside to build a snowman," Ross whispered, his hand pressing on hers.

"What a wonderful idea." Sage leaned over, kissed his navel, then jumped out of bed when her son yelled again through the doors. She snatched at her robe, aware that Ross had pulled the covers up to his hips and was lying on his side watching her every move. She threw open the door to the hall of the suite, wishing that she didn't redden when she looked down into the bright-eyed face of her son, his sister at his side.

"Yo-u didn't he-ar me." Tad grinned at her toothily.

"I knocked too," Pip told her, each word rapped out like a nail on wood.

"You did?" Sage felt teary as she ushered the children into the room.

Ross was sitting up on the bed, Indian fashion, dressed in silk pajama bottoms only. He opened his arms to the children and they ran and jumped on the bed.

The three of them wrestled for a few minutes, tumbling and laughing, Sage watching them.

When Ross finally sat up, his hair rumpled, his cheeks flushed, he had a child under each arm, holding them close to him.

"Tell Daddy what you said, Pippa," Sage directed the child quietly, facing Tad so that he could read her lips.

Tad nodded, jostling his sister gently. "Go-o on."

Pip swallowed and looked at Ross solemnly. "I knocked on the door too."

When Sage saw Ross's face sag in delight she felt a wetness on her cheeks.

"That's wonderful, angel," Ross told the little girl huskily, pulling her onto his lap and hugging her, then turning to hug Tad. "I am so very proud of both of you. You make me very happy." He choked, then bent his head over the two of them.

Sage stood there, threading and unthreading her hands, not able to stem the tears that flowed from her eyes. She looked around her, expecting to see the moon entering the window, stars pasted to the ceiling of the room. Instead her eye caught on the time. "Lord, it's almost cocktail time."

Pip pushed at her brother and finger-spelled.

"Oh-h, yes. El-sie said we were to tell yo-ou to get dressed." He grinned and jumped down from the bed. "We are staying with Gr-ampa and Gr-amma when you go to the other house and we're go-ing to do lots of things." He looked at his sister. "Pi-ip!" he shouted.

"*We're* ready," Pip told her father primly, making Ross shout with glee.

"Lord, I'm getting another nagging woman."

The children left the room on the run, saying they were going downstairs with Elsie.

Sage ran over and jumped on the bed, pushing Ross flat when he would have risen. "What was that remark about another nagging woman?"

"Did I say that?"

"You did." She held his hands on the bed, straddling him.

"Ummmm, lovely. If this is *punishment*, I want more," he murmured, undulating under her.

"Pervert," she whispered, nipping at his lip with her teeth. "And that's for calling me a nag."

"I can think of other names," Ross told her, his eyes closed. "Do your worst."

Several lights on the phone console went on, catching Sage's attention.

Ross flipped her easily onto her back, covering her with his body. "So punish me, lady."

"Too late." Sage loosened one hand that he was holding and pointed to the console. "We're wanted."

Ross glared at the message light. "I'm taking you away to Tahiti." He rolled off the bed and pulled her with him.

"But can you paint, Gauguin?" she said from the side of her mouth as she lifted the receiver. "Yes? Of course. We'll come right away." She hung up. "That was—"

"I don't want to hear." A disgruntled Ross gave her a baleful look when she laughed.

Ross pushed open the door of the capacious two-story library, faces and voices assaulting him and Sage at the same moment.

"It's about time." His sister Leslie glided up to them. "Second honeymoon?"

Ross looked down his nose at her, but she only tinkled a laugh.

"Sage, darling, you can't be still blushing after all these years," Leslie continued.

"Only when she's around you."

"Ross, don't be a boor," Leslie rounded on her brother.

"Back off, Les." Slater came up to his wife and winked at Sage.

Leslie shrugged, looking at Sage challengingly.

Sage studied her for a moment, then started to laugh. "I'm sorry, but it's so funny that you would have to ask what we were doing when we were alone." Sage shot a quick glance at the children clustered around the piano and singing to Will's inexpert playing. "Can you have forgotten?"

Ross's chuckle and Slater's smothered laugh were a background for Leslie's gasp.

Sage stood there, chin up, watching her sister-in-law. When she saw her lips quiver, then a chuckle escape them, she felt as though she had been hit with a cattle prod.

"Sooo, the little girl fights back at last," Leslie murmured, her smile widening. "And I haven't forgotten anything. Have I, Slater?"

"No, ma'am." He kissed his wife's cheek, then leaned forward to kiss Sage. "And how are you, baby sister?"

"Not such a baby anymore," Leslie murmured.

"Just fine, Slater. Better and better." Sage heard the surprised realization in her voice.

"You look great. By the way, did I tell you Sinj has been a bear since you left?" Slater spoke with the brass of a former university roommate, smiling blandly at his teeth-baring friend. "Going to fire me as the company lawyer?"

"Kill you."

"Neither one." Leslie poked Ross's arm. "Slater is right. You've been a Tartar for months." She turned to Sage. "I could tell you—"

"Sage isn't interested," Ross said abruptly, taking his wife's arm and leading her toward the center of the room, where two long cream silk couches faced each other over a huge glass coffee table and were perpendicular to the Adams fireplace. "Mother. Father." Ross kept Sage close to him.

"In a temper, Sinjon?" His mother paused in the act of lifting a wineglass to her mouth.

"No," Ross snapped. "Ma'am," he added bitingly.

"Fit o' pique," his sister Barbara explained blandly, settling back on the couch. "Does he have dyspepsia? I don't know what that is exactly, but I think Scrooge had it. Or was that gout? Of course I don't know what they are, but I understand when you're grouchy like Sinjon that could be the cause."

Sage bit her lip to contain the mirth bubbling in her.

"You're wise not to laugh, sweetheart," Ross acknowledged, his arm tightening on her quivering form.

Sage chuckled up at him. "I never fully appreciated your family's sense of comedy."

Ross's eyes glinted in icy humor. "You're pretty funny yourself."

"Yes." Sage leaned over and bit his cheek just as he was taking a swallow of Irish whiskey, neat. "I'm discovering hidden depths in myself."

Ross swallowed the whiskey and stared at her. "Are you, now?"

As though a button had been pushed, the others were silent.

Sage looked around her, feeling an alien serenity. Confidence wasn't flowing through her, but there was definitely a seepage into her system. Her spine seemed to straighten, her chin lifted. She stared at her husband. "How about that?"

"Remarkable." Ross felt amused irritation building in him. His spring rose really was turning into a flowering cactus! Was she going to take on the entire clan? And she could, he answered his own question. Quiet delight filled him as he watched her adjust herself more comfortably opposite his mother. She looked prim and incredibly sexy all at the same time in her man-tailored silk.

Glasses clinked with ice, conversation resumed, though there were many surprised looks cast at Sage.

"Mom-my, play the pi-ano." Tad grinned at everyone.

"If you like." Sage rose to her feet. "Do you want to sing?" She spoke to Tad but she managed to encompass all the children in her look.

"Can he do that?" Heppie rose to her feet, carrying her wineglass and walking next to Sage as they approached the piano. "Hear you, I mean?"

Sage shook her head, smiling at Jorge, who had pulled the piano stool out for her. "He can't hear, but he can keep time. The doctors have told me that because Tad is such an intelligent youngster, he has worked out a system of 'listening' all his own. He feels the vibrations from the piano and picks up the rhythm. Hearing-impaired people are amazing," she told her mother-in-law proudly.

"Tad is, of course. He's like all the Tempests," Heppie informed her.

"Brilliant," Barbara stated, frowning at her husband, Barry, when he guffawed. "Well, look at our two. Debbie and Will are very good in school."

"That comes from my side," Barry told her, kissing her lips when she would have protested. "Shhh. Sage is going to play. Incidentally, little sister, I didn't know you were musical."

"She never liked to play in front of anyone, but she used to practice at home," Ross pointed out, not adding that he hadn't heard her play since the early months of their marriage.

Her head shot up and she stared at him as though she'd read his mind. "I hadn't wanted to play in a long time, but when I went back to Irondequoit I played every day just to keep my mind off . . ." Sage's voice trailed away. She looked away from Ross, smiled at Jorge, and shook her head when he asked her if she would like him to push her bench closer to the piano.

Tad had Pip by the hand as he wriggled through the gathering group of adults clustering near the concert grand. "Si-ing 'Danny Boy.' " He turned to Jorge, who was close to him. "But Mom si-ings Taddy Boy." He chortled when Jorge laughed.

Sage flexed her fingers, running them up and down the keyboard. Then she nodded at the boy, who was watching her and the instrument intently. She was on the second verse when Pip joined her, the child's tremolo voice surprisingly rich and true.

Ross touched Tad's arm and indicated Pip.

When the boy turned to look at his sister, Sage went into the intro again and nodded at the little girl, whose eyes were shining.

Pip took a deep breath and sang. ". . . and when you kneel and tell me that you love me, I will sleep in peace until you come to me." The child's voice rose on the last note, holding it sweetly.

"Pip-pa." Tad shook her arm and grinned.

"Darling," Sage sobbed, lifting one hand toward the child.

"Daddy's sweetheart." Ross caught the little child up in his arms, his voice breaking. "So beautiful."

Pip hugged Ross, and it was as though they and Sage and Tad were alone, dancing on the stars.

Eleven

Thanksgiving Day dawned cold and crisp. Some of the snowdrifts reached to the second floor on the windy corners of the great house.

Sage opened her eyes and looked at the alarm clock. It would go off at seven and it was now six-thirty. She came wider awake, aware of the heaviness on her waist. She knew it was Ross's arm without turning to look at him. She squeezed her eyes shut and moved a fraction closer so that his warm skin touched her from shoulder to ankle. Only he had the power to make her feel secure, relaxed, yet at the same time irritated and out of balance. She sighed and decided she would get up earlier than planned. Sage edged away from Ross's form.

"No," Ross mumbled, snatching her back to him, his arm imprisoning her. "Kiss me," he said softly, his eyes shut.

"Have we met?" Sage was relieved he didn't seem as

uptight with her as he had been since their arrival at Highgate.

"Briefly," Ross told her, running his mouth over her shoulder, pushing aside the strap of her nightgown. "I undressed you last night and put you to bed." He opened his eyes and leered at her. "And nice work it was too."

"Are you the one who walked through my dreams telling me that I was staying with him on a desert island?"

"Don't be silly." Ross knew his voice was too abrupt. Her subconscious had retained what he had said to her last night! The words he had crooned to her while undressing her had lodged in a cranny of her mind!

Sage could feel her mouth falling open! Ross Tempest blushing, looking discomfited! Had the moon fallen out of its place in the firmament? What was causing him to fidget? Sage smothered a yawn and looked at the clock. "Lord. It's almost seven. I have to go." She catapulted out of bed before Ross could tighten his grip again.

"Wait a minute. I'll shower with you," he called to her even as she slammed the bathroom door. He gnashed his teeth when he heard the lock turn. "Sage!" he bellowed, jumping out of bed and striding nude to the bathroom door.

She chuckled. "Use the other shower. I'm in a hurry. Time to stuff the turkey."

"Stuff it up a chimney," he rasped, shaking the doorknob. "Let me in."

"No." She turned on the shower in the roomy stall that stood next to the round sunken tub, feeling a childish glee that Ross Tempest was standing on the other side of the door banging to get in there with her. "Tough buns, big fella." She laughed aloud and drowned out his voice in the cascading water. She took the time to shampoo her hair and spend a few minutes in the sauna.

It was while she was supine in the wooden enclosure that she thought she heard the sound of hammering, but she paid no attention, knowing that she had a scant ten minutes before she had to take a cool-off shower, dress, and get down to the kitchen. She was dozing when the door to the cubicle opened and Ross was there on the slatted bench next to her. "How . . . how—"

"I removed the hinges on the door," he explained, lifting her and placing his body under her. "I don't want you to bruise your body on the wood."

"You're crazy." She gulped, looking down at him. "Those are heavy oak doors. They're too much for one man."

"Not one desperate man who needed your softness," he muttered, pulling her face down to his and undulating under her. "And for goodness' sake don't tell me we don't have time for a cuddle!"

"We have time for a cuddle." She surrendered, wanting him to hold her, needing him, wanting him more than she wanted to breathe. The acceptance of that shuddered through her, making her clutch him.

"What's wrong, Sage?" Ross embraced her. "Are you ill? You're shivering."

"It's not fair. You shouldn't have come into my life again." She exhaled.

He shot to a sitting position with her still in his arms, hurt pulsing through him at her words. "Listen to me." He fired the words from his mouth. "I'm in your life for the distance. Nothing will change that."

"Things change," she told him dully, still in shock at what she had admitted to herself. "Have to get cooking."

"I'll work with you." He dumped her onto her feet, his teeth clamped together. He felt like turning her upside down and paddling her until she turned bright red for being so stubborn. It took all his concentration not to do it.

Sage barely glanced at him when she left the sauna at a gallop. She was tearfully grateful that she had the worry and fretting of preparing the Thanksgiving dinner.

Dashing down the three flights of back stairway, she heard Ross call to her. She paused and looked over her shoulder.

"I'll join you in a minute. I want to check on the children and make sure that Elsie is with them." He disappeared from the top of the stairs.

She stood frozen in her tracks. She had again forgotten all about her children in the frenzy of emotion she experienced about Ross. Lord, he was going to drive her insane. Maybe she was there already, she thought on a quiver of hysteria.

The family dressed like Eskimos for the annual football game, heavily swaddling the children.

"I don't know how we'll find the ball if it goes in the drifts," Jorge told Sage as they chose sides. He would be playing on Ross's team. She would play on Slater's.

Sage shrugged. "Not to worry. The Tempests always have answers for everything."

The game began and in minutes they were laughing, shouting, and charging around, the children as well as the adults.

Ross saw Sage catch the ball and come plowing down through the snow laughing, her cheeks red, Tad hotfooting it after her to catch her. When Jorge rushed toward her, Ross cut in front of the man, causing him to stumble. Then he tackled Sage himself, catching her so that she fell on top of him.

"Cheater." Sage tried to push his face in the snow.

"If that's what it takes to keep you, yes." He lifted her up and wiped the snow from her. "Anything I have to do." He leaped away from her, calling to his team to scramble.

Sage looked after him, feeling all at sea, out of balance.

The game ended with Ross's team winning.

"Did you doubt that he would win?" Barbara sighed. "He always played harder than anyone I ever knew."

"And still does." Jorge flexed a shoulder.

Ross ambled up to them, tossing the ball in the air. "Oh, Mendez. I called up one of the neighbors. Phyllis Leeds. She's going to be your dinner companion today," Ross told him blandly. "She and her father and uncle will be joining us for dinner."

"I didn't know that." Heppie shook the snow off her clothes as they all went into the locker room that opened off the yard. "Not that I mind. I like all the Leeds."

"Nice surprise." Joshua's eyes glinted at his son.

"I think so."

"And I think I understand." Jorge looked at him.

"I thought you might." Ross was unsmiling.

Sage was going to say something but her brothers-in-law took her arms and led her away.

"When Sinj is in one of his moods, he'll tolerate you, Sage, and no one else, but I think this is one of those rare times when everyone should give him a wide berth," Barry told her, grinning over her head at Slater.

"If you think for one minute that Ross can intimidate me—"

"We don't think that, Sage," Slater soothed. "It's just that we realize that he's at the end of his tether. Shouldn't we be looking at the turkeys?"

"Good Lord, yes." Sage broke free of her in-laws and sprinted for the kitchen, all thoughts of Ross wiped from her mind at the moment.

Dinner was a huge success, with Joshua carving one turkey at the head of the table and Ross carving the other at the foot. The large electric hot table on the sideboard that had the appearance of an ornate tray kept everything piping hot.

It surprised Sage how eagerly her sisters-in-law tackled the job of serving the children while she passed the vegetables. It was even more of a stunner when they were all able to sit down at the same time, ask the blessing, and eat.

"Ummm. My dear child, this is the best turkey we've ever had." Joshua beamed at his wife when she nodded and smiled. "And the dressing . . ."

"And vegetables that my darling wife prepared." Barry kissed Barbara.

"And mine." Slater hugged Leslie. "And it's been fun. I agree with Heppie. We should make this an annual event. Give the help time off and we'll do it."

"I think that's a splendid idea," Sage told her in-laws quietly, not looking at Ross when she sensed his glance shooting her way.

The pies, ice cream, and strawberries Romanoff were greeted with groans and sighs.

"We could just have coffee and the strawberries now and save the pies for later," Sage suggested, receiving enthusiastic agreement on that.

The women let the men and children clear the table while they began rinsing and stacking the dishes in the dishwashers.

"My goodness, that didn't take long and now we can enjoy our dessert." Heppie looked pleased as they sat down again at the long dining-room table that could seat sixty with all the leaves inserted. "Sinjon, why are you glowering at your strawberries? Surely the Grand Marnier is to your liking."

A muscle jumped at the side of his mouth, "Sage and I will be leaving to stay in the gardener's cottage overnight and—"

"Wonderful. I shall put the children in the bedrooms

near our suite. They're larger anyway." She looked at the children. "You would like to sleep in a room near Grandmother and Grandfather, wouldn't you?"

Tad nodded eagerly. He had become close to all his relatives in the short time he had been with them. Pip was more reticent, but she nodded also.

"That's settled."

Pip smiled at her mother and nodded as though to an unspoken question.

"Lovely." Heppie basked in the contentment of her household. "You are a genius, dear Sage. I fully intend to go to Irondequoit and work in your restaurant. I enjoyed this." She frowned when Leslie whispered. "Oh, oh, there goes the business." Her forehead cleared. "Is Irondequoit near a city? Like Yonkers, perhaps?"

"Rochester, Mother," Ross said.

"Ohhh. Yes, I know that city. They have a great deal of snow."

"I like sno-ow." Tad smiled at his grandmother.

She smiled back at him indulgently.

Ross rose and moved to Sage's chair. "You're finished with dessert. Mother will marshal the troops here." He practically lifted her from her seat.

"But—"

"Bye, Mommy." Tad read Ross's lips, and now he smiled at Sage cheerfully.

"Bye," Pip said softly.

"But . . . my children . . ."

"*Our* children," Ross corrected her, shepherding her toward the door.

"Not to worry, Sage. They'll play with ours," Barry told her happily.

"But—"

"See you tomorrow, Sage." Joshua waved his hand, his eyes twinkling.

Sage was out of the room and in the foyer before she could formulate an argument.

Ross pushed her into a parka and sat her in a Louis Quinze chair to put on her boots. "Let's go. There's food down there and other clothing we might need."

Sage stared at him. "This is too fast. Besides, I'll never eat again." She tried to free herself from his grip as he led her out the front door. "How did you get this organized? How do you know there's food? Not that we need it. . . ." she babbled, looking around her wildly. "My goodness, it's snowing again," she finished lamely, letting him lead her down the drive that curved through the woods to the road. The cottage was close to the man-made lake on the property that had been used for duck hunting in years gone by, but was now used for summer canoeing.

"We have to talk, Sage. Don't you think it's about time?"

"Yes."

Ross began to run along the slippery drive, pulling her with him. "We don't have that much time before the world intrudes again. Hurry."

When he slipped again and was off balance, Sage threw her body sideways, causing him to stumble into a snowdrift at the side of the road. He fell backward, his arms flailing, causing Sage to whoop with laughter. "You look so funny." Even as she said it she saw the glint in his eye. She started running before he had struggled to his feet, knowing that Tempest was on her heels.

Ross watched her run ahead of him, impressed by the long, strong stride, not doubting for a moment he could catch her, but pleased to have her get to the cottage that much faster by running. When she flung herself at the front door and it opened, he redoubled his speed just in time to throw himself on the closing door. "Oh no, you don't, darling. Run if you must, but you can't escape me. That I won't allow."

Sage fell back laughing, opening her mittened hand and throwing a handful of snow at him even as he came through the door.

"Brat." He lifted her up, kicking the door shut and carrying her to the couch that sat in front of the fireplace of the living and dining room. He sat down with her in his lap, undoing her parka. "If I had several days alone with you, I'd take you out in the snow and wash your face in it—"

"Not without a fight."

"And then I'd build you a snowman with eyes and a nose . . ." He peeled the coat from her, throwing it on a chair, following it with her gloves and hat. "Then I would bring you in here and offer you"—he felt the smile fall off his face—"no, beg you, to take my life and intertwine it with yours forever." He moved her to one side on the couch, to divest himself of his own coat. He didn't take his eyes from her. "I love you, Sagacity. I have loved you for a long, long time. I need you in my life to give it depth, color, excitement, serenity . . . and joy, and Tad and Pip are part of that."

Sage stared at him, inhaling a shaky breath, her eyes stinging with the emotional love that had begun building inside her from the moment she had met Ross St. John Tempest. "It has hurt to love you," she said huskily.

"But you do?" All his vital signs closed down waiting for the answer.

"I don't want to . . . but I do."

Ross bent over her hand, placing his face in the palm. "Nothing has ever mattered so much."

Sage placed her hand on his head, loving the feel of the strong skull under her hand. "We have to have rules . . . like the Marquis of Queensberry, I think."

"Darling, I don't want to box with you. Wrestle, yes." Ross pressed his lips into her palm.

"Ross, do we have a chance?"

"Together, yes. Apart, there's no chance for me." He lifted his head. "I love you, Sage. You're my blood and flesh. If you cut me out, I'll keep moving, but I'll be dead," he told her in low tones. "I need you and the children. I have never been more frightened than when you left me and I thought it might be for good."

"The world will intrude."

"Nothing will come between us."

"Speaking of children, I thought we were going to work on having one of our own."

Ross had droll amusement in his eyes. "It will take a great deal of work, I think."

"A commitment, maybe?"

"Could be." He pushed her back on the couch and knelt at her side. "Tell me you'll stay with me."

"I love you, Tempest. I have to stay."

Ross gasped and buried his face in her neck. Later he would make love to her with a dedication and fervor that told her more than words that their love was for all time.

THE EDITOR'S CORNER

First to last, you've got a zippy month of LOVE-SWEPT reading ahead with our next four romances that will take you all the way from the Casa Grande Retirement Center to the casbah in Sedikhan!

We start with a fabulous love story by much-loved author Sara Orwig, **UNDER THE GINKGO TREE,** LOVESWEPT #123. Young and lovely Sandy Smith is the manager of a retirement center and she has a problem on the grounds: the ginkgo trees have wilted ... for the third time! Nursery owner Gabe London can't believe that his healthy trees have a survival rate of zero, so he decides he has to do a little detective work. Then he meets Sandy. And right away he's fairly certain what pest is attacking the ginkgos—his younger brother who has a terrible crush on the beautiful, warm-hearted manager. After all, Gabe reasons, what red-blooded male, young or old, wouldn't want an excuse to hang around Sandy? He does. So he comes up with an ingenious scheme ... one that provides lots of chuckles and sizzle on a bumpy road to happily-ever-after!

The next stop on the LOVESWEPT route next month is Washington, D.C. and the wonderfully emotional love story, **BANJO MAN,** LOVESWEPT #124 by Adrienne Staff and Sally Goldenbaum. Hero Rick Westin is a breathtakingly tender human being and a gifted musician. And the moment he lays eyes on incredibly innocent and totally honest Laurie McNeill he is a goner! But Laurie's life has been so sheltered that he must proceed with great care in his wooing of her. And

(continued)

she must use all her courage and sense of humor to cope with the new world into which she has emerged. A hauntingly lovely story, **BANJO MAN** is every bit as unique as Adrienne's and Sally's first LOVESWEPT, **WHAT'S A NICE GIRL ...?** about which so many of you wrote glowing letters.

Husband-and-wife writing team Anne and Ed Kolaczyk are back, too, with their second romance for us, **ORANGES IN THE SNOW**, LOVESWEPT #125. In this witty, heartstoppingly sensual love story, you'll meet a transplanted California girl trying to cope with a new job, a new life under the arctic conditions of one of Minnesota's coldest winters on record. Ah, but from the first, when she's stranded in a blizzard, she's got a great big, sweetheart of a man who wants to keep her warm! Like a bearded Viking of old, Per Nielsen sets out to conquer the heart of the lady from the warmer clime by showing her all the delights possible in the chilly north. In his march toward victory, he gets some help from a couple of outcast kittens, a mysterious female named Freya ... and quite a bit of hindrance from an old-fashioned device called the "bundling board" and a parent's legacy that was misunderstood until almost too late. As invigorating as a romp in the snow and as juicy as California's famous oranges, this romance lives up to the promise of its title, so don't miss **ORANGES IN THE SNOW**.

Keeping a tiger cub in the house was tame stuff compared to what a grown up Pandora Madchen has in store for Philip El Kabbar in Iris Johansen's next romance **AND THE DESERT BLOOMS**, LOVESWEPT #126. Six years after the close of **A SUMMER SMILE**, we rediscover

Pandora on tour in San Francisco as a rock star . . . and about to launch a devious, long-planned scheme. Her first moves are certainly successful and bring Philip at a run to her from Sedikhan. But once she has ensnared him, he proves almost too much for her . . . until, returning to his home, she finds a way to touch the heart of his emotions as no one ever has before. Another thoroughly delightful, entrancingly passionate tale from Iris, whose "family" of characters has become so cherished by us all.

Everyone at LOVESWEPT wishes you a New Year filled with all the best things in life—peace, prosperity, and the love of family and friends.

Sincerely,

Carolyn Nichols

Carolyn Nichols
   Editor
LOVESWEPT
Bantam Books, Inc.
666 Fifth Avenue
New York, NY 10103

 # LOVESWEPT

Love Stories you'll never forget by authors you'll always remember

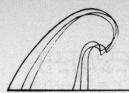

LOVESWEPT

Love Stories you'll never forget by authors you'll always remember

Prices and availability subject to change without notice.

Buy them at your local bookstore or use this handy coupon for ordering:

LOVESWEPT

Love Stories you'll never forget by authors you'll always remember

Prices and availability subject to change without notice.

Buy them at your local bookstore or use this handy coupon for ordering: